I guess I should explain. I'm not exactly your typical sixteen-year-old girl.

Oh, I *seem* normal enough, I guess. I don't do drugs, or drink, or smoke—well, okay, except for that one time when my stepbrother caught me. I don't have anything pierced, except my ears, and only once on each earlobe. I don't have any tattoos. I've never dyed my hair. Except for my boots and leather jacket, I don't wear an excessive amount of black. I don't even wear dark fingernail polish. All in all, I am a pretty normal, everyday, American teenage girl.

Except, of course, for the fact that I can talk to the dead.

## *Books by Meg Cabot*

THE MEDIATOR 1: SHADOWLAND
THE MEDIATOR 2: NINTH KEY
THE MEDIATOR 3: REUNION
THE MEDIATOR 4: DARKEST HOUR
THE MEDIATOR 5: HAUNTED
THE MEDIATOR 6: TWILIGHT

THE PRINCESS DIARIES
THE PRINCESS DIARIES, VOLUME II: PRINCESS IN THE SPOTLIGHT
THE PRINCESS DIARIES, VOLUME III: PRINCESS IN LOVE
THE PRINCESS DIARIES, VOLUME IV: PRINCESS IN WAITING
THE PRINCESS DIARIES, VOLUME IV AND A HALF: PROJECT PRINCESS
THE PRINCESS DIARIES, VOLUME V: PRINCESS IN PINK
THE PRINCESS DIARIES, VOLUME VI: PRINCESS IN TRAINING
THE PRINCESS PRESENT: A PRINCESS DIARIES BOOK
PRINCESS LESSONS: A PRINCESS DIARIES BOOK
PERFECT PRINCESS: A PRINCESS DIARIES BOOK

ALL-AMERICAN GIRL
TEEN IDOL
NICOLA AND THE VISCOUNT
VICTORIA AND THE ROGUE
THE BOY NEXT DOOR
BOY MEETS GIRL
EVERY BOY'S GOT ONE

THE 1-800-WHERE-R-YOU BOOKS:
WHEN LIGHTNING STRIKES
CODE NAME CASSANDRA
SAFE HOUSE
SANCTUARY

# MEG CABOT

# the mediator
## Shadowland

avon books
AN IMPRINT OF HARPERCOLLINS*PUBLISHERS*

The Mediator: Shadowland

Originally published in 2000 by Simon Pulse,
an imprint of Simon & Schuster, Inc.
 Printed in the United States of America. For information address HarperCollins Children's Books, a division of HarperCollins Publishers, 1350 Avenue of the Americas, New York, NY 10019.

Library of Congress Catalog Card Number: 2004093412
ISBN 0-06-072511-7
First Avon edition, 2005



❖

Visit us on the World Wide Web!
www.megcabot.com
www.harperteen.com

*In memory of A. Victor Cabot,*

*and his brother, Jack "France" Cabot*

# chapter one

They told me there'd be palm trees.

I didn't believe them, but that's what they told me. They told me I'd be able to see them from the plane.

Oh, I know they have palm trees in southern California. I mean, I'm not a complete moron. I've watched *90210*, and everything. But I was moving to northern California. I didn't expect to see palm trees in northern California. Not after my mom told me not to give away all my sweaters.

"Oh, no," my mom had said. "You'll need them. Your coats, too. It can get cold there. Not as cold as New York, maybe, but pretty chilly."

Which was why I wore my black leather motorcycle jacket on the plane. I could have shipped it, I guess, with the rest of my stuff, but it kind of made me feel better to wear it.

So there I was, sitting on the plane in a black leather motorcycle jacket, seeing these palm trees through the window as we landed. And I thought, Great. Black leather and palm trees. Already I'm fitting in, just like I knew I would. . . .

. . . *Not.*

My mom isn't particularly fond of my leather jacket, but I swear I didn't wear it to make her mad, or anything. I'm not resentful of the fact that she decided to marry a guy who lives three thousand miles away, forcing me to leave school in the middle of my sophomore year; abandon the best—and pretty much only—friend I've had since kindergarten; leave the city I've been living in for all of my sixteen years.

Oh, no. I'm not a bit resentful.

The thing is, I really do like Andy, my new stepdad. He's good for my mom. He makes her happy. And he's very nice to me.

It's just this moving-to-California thing that bugs me.

Oh, and did I mention Andy's three other kids?

They were all there to greet me when I got off

the plane. My mom, Andy, and Andy's three sons. Sleepy, Dopey, and Doc, I call them. They're my new stepbrothers.

"Susie!" Even if I hadn't heard my mom squealing my name as I walked through the gate, I wouldn't have missed them—my new family. Andy was making his two youngest boys hold up this big sign that said WELCOME HOME, SUSANNAH! Everybody getting off my flight was walking by it, going, "Aw, look how cute," to their travel companions, and smiling at me in this sickening way.

Oh, yeah. I'm fitting in. I'm fitting in just great.

"Okay," I said, walking up to my new family fast. "You can put the sign down now."

But my mom was too busy hugging me to pay any attention. "Oh, Susie!" she kept saying. I hate when anybody but my mom calls me Susie, so I shot the boys this mean look over her shoulder, just in case they were getting any big ideas. They just kept grinning at me from over the stupid sign, Dopey because he's too dumb to know any better, Doc because—well, I guess because he might have been glad to see me. Doc's weird that way. Sleepy, the oldest, just stood there, looking . . . well, sleepy.

"How was your flight, kiddo?" Andy took my bag off my shoulder, and put it on his own. He seemed surprised by how heavy it was, and went, "Whoa, what've you got in here, anyway? You know it's a felony to smuggle New York City fire hydrants across state lines."

I smiled at him. Andy's this really big goof, but he's a nice big goof. He wouldn't have the slightest idea what constitutes a felony in the state of New York since he's only been there, like, five times. Which was, incidentally, exactly how many visits it took him to convince my mother to marry him.

"It's not a fire hydrant," I said. "It's a parking meter. And I have four more bags."

"Four?" Andy pretended he was shocked. "What do you think you're doing, moving in or something?"

Did I mention that Andy thinks he's a comedian? He's not. He's a carpenter.

"Suze," Doc said, all enthusiastically. "Suze, did you notice that as you were landing, the tail of the plane kicked up a little? That was from an updraft. It's caused when a mass moving at a considerable rate of speed encounters a counter-blowing wind velocity of equal or greater strength."

Doc, Andy's youngest kid, is twelve, but he's going on about forty. He spent almost the entire wedding reception telling me about alien cattle mutilation, and how Area 51 is just this big cover-up by the American government, which doesn't want us to know that We Are Not Alone.

"Oh, Susie," my mom kept saying. "I'm so glad you're here. You're just going to love the house. It just didn't feel like home at first, but now that you're here . . . Oh, and wait until you've seen your room. Andy's fixed it up so nice. . . ."

Andy and my mom spent weeks before they got married looking for a house big enough for all four kids to have their own rooms. They finally settled on this huge house in the hills of Carmel, which they'd only been able to afford because they'd bought it in this completely wretched state, and this construction company Andy does a lot of work for fixed it up at this big discount rate. My mom has been going on for days about my room, which she keeps swearing is the nicest one in the house.

"The view!" she kept saying. "An ocean view from the big bay window in your room! Oh, Suze, you're going to love it."

I was sure I was going to love it. About as much as I was going to love giving up bagels for alfalfa sprouts, and the subway for surfing, and all that sort of stuff.

For some reason, Dopey opened his mouth, and went, "Do you like the sign?" in that stupid voice of his. I can't believe he's my age. He's on the school wrestling team, though, so what can you expect? All he ever thinks about, from what I could tell when I had to sit next to him at the wedding reception—I had to sit between him and Doc, so you can imagine how the conversation just flowed—is choke holds and body-building protein shakes.

"Yeah, great sign," I said, yanking it out of his meaty hands, and holding it so that the lettering faced the floor. "Can we go? I wanna pick up my bags before someone else does."

"Oh, right," my mom said. She gave me one last hug. "Oh, I'm just so glad to see you! You look so great. . . ." And then, even though you could tell she didn't want to say it, she went ahead and said it anyway, in a low voice, so no one else could hear: "Thought I've talked to you before about that jacket, Suze. And I thought you were throwing those jeans away."

I was wearing my oldest jeans, the ones with the holes in the knees. They went really well with my black silk T and my zip-up ankle boots. The jeans and boots, coupled with my black leather motorcycle jacket and my Army-Navy surplus shoulder bag, made me look like a teen runaway in a made-for-TV movie.

But hey, when you're flying for eight hours across the country, you want to be comfortable.

I said that, and my mom just rolled her eyes and dropped it. That's the good thing about my mom. She doesn't harp, like other moms do. Sleepy, Dopey, and Doc have no idea how lucky they are.

"All right," she said, instead. "Let's get your bags." Then, raising her voice, she called, "Jake, come on. We're going to get Suze's bags."

She had to call Sleepy by name, since he looked as if he had fallen asleep standing up. I asked my mother once if Jake, who is a senior in high school, has narcolepsy, or possibly a drug habit, and she was like, "No, why would you say that?" Like the guy doesn't just stand there blinking all the time, never saying a word to anyone.

Wait, that's not true. He did say something to me, once. Once he said, "Hey, are you in a gang?" He asked me that at the wedding, when he caught me standing outside with my leather jacket on over my maid of honor's dress, sneaking a cigarette.

Give me a break, all right? It was my first and only cigarette ever. I was under a lot of stress at the time. I was worried my mom was going to marry this guy and move to California and forget all about me. I swear I haven't smoked a single cigarette since.

And don't get me wrong about Jake. At six foot one, with the same shaggy blond hair and twinkly blue eyes as his dad, he's what my best friend Gina would call a hottie. But he's not the shiniest rock in the rock garden, if you know what I mean.

Doc was still going on about wind velocity. He was explaining the speed with which it is necessary to travel in order to break through the earth's gravitational force. This speed is called escape velocity. I decided Doc might be useful to have around, homework-wise, even if I am three grades ahead of him.

While Doc talked, I looked around. This was my first trip ever to California, and let me tell you, even though we were still only in the airport—and it was the San Jose International Airport—you could tell we weren't in New York anymore. I mean, first off, everything was clean. No dirt, no litter, no graffiti anywhere. The concourse was all done up in pastels, too, and you know how light colors show the dirt. Why do you think New Yorkers wear black all the time? Not to be cool. Nuh-uh. So we don't have to haul all our clothes down to the Laundromat every single time we wear them.

But that didn't appear to be a problem in sunny CA. From what I could tell, pastels were in. This one woman walked by us, and she had on pink leggings and a white Spandex sports bra. And that's all. If this is an example of what's *de rigueur* in California, I could tell I was in for some major culture shock.

And you know what else was strange? Nobody was fighting. There were passengers lined up here and there, but they weren't raising their voices at the people behind the ticket counter. In New York, if you're a customer, you fight with the people behind the counter, no matter where you are—airport, Bloomingdale's, hot dog stand. Wherever.

Not here. Everybody here was just way calm.

And I guess I could see why. I mean, it didn't look to me like there was anything to get upset about. Outside, the sun was beating down on those palm trees I'd seen from the sky. There were seagulls—not pigeons, but actual big white-and-gray seagulls—scratching around in the parking lot. And when we went to get my bags, nobody even checked to see if the stickers on them matched my ticket stubs. No, everybody was just like, "Buh-bye! Have a nice day!"

Unreal.

Gina—she was my best friend back in Brooklyn; well, okay, my *only* friend, really—told me before I left that I'd find there were advantages to having three stepbrothers. She should know since she's got four—not steps, but real brothers. Anyway, I didn't believe her any more than I'd believed people about the palm trees. But when Sleepy picked up two of my bags, and Dopey grabbed the other two, leaving me with exactly nothing to carry, since Andy had my shoulder bag, I finally realized what she was talking about: Brothers can be useful. They can carry really heavy stuff, and not even look like it's bothering them.

Hey, I packed those bags. I knew what was in them. They were not light. But Sleepy and Dopey were like, No problem here. Let's get moving.

My bags secure, we headed out into the parking lot. As the automatic doors opened, everyone—including my mom—reached into a pocket and pulled out a pair of sunglasses. Apparently, they all knew something I didn't know. And as I stepped outside, I realized what it was.

It's *sunny* here.

Not just sunny, either, but bright—so bright and colorful, it hurts your eyes. I had sunglasses, too, somewhere, but since it had been about forty degrees and sleeting when I left New York, I hadn't thought to put them anywhere easily accessible. When my mother had first told me we'd be moving—she and Andy decided it was easier for her, with one kid and a job as a TV news reporter, to relocate than it would be for Andy and his three kids to do it, especially considering that Andy owns his own business—she'd explained to me that I'd love northern California. "It's where they filmed all those Goldie Hawn, Chevy Chase movies!" she told me.

I like Goldie Hawn, and I like Chevy Chase, but I never knew they made a movie together.

"It's where all those Steinbeck stories you had to read in school took place," she said. "You know, *The Red Pony*."

Well, I wasn't very impressed. I mean, all I remembered from *The Red Pony* was that there weren't any girls in it, although there were a lot of hills. And as I stood in the parking lot, squinting at the hills surrounding the San Jose International Airport, I saw that there were a lot of hills, and the grass on them was dry and brown.

But dotting the hills were these trees, trees not like any I'd ever seen before. They were squashed on top as if a giant fist had come down from the sky and given them a thump. I found out later these were called cypress trees.

And all around the parking lot, where there was evidently a watering system, there were these fat bushes with these giant red flowers on them, mostly squatting down at the bottom of these impossibly tall, surprisingly thick palm trees. The flowers, I found out, when I looked them up later, were hibiscus. And the strange-looking bugs that I saw hovering around them, making a *brrr*-ing noise, weren't bugs at all. They were humming-birds.

"Oh," my mom said when I pointed this out. "They're everywhere. We have feeders for them up at the house. You can hang one from your window if you want."

Hummingbirds that come right up to your window? The only birds that ever came up to my window back in Brooklyn were pigeons. My mom never exactly encouraged me to feed them.

My moment of joy about the hummingbirds was shattered when Dopey announced suddenly, "I'll drive," and started for the driver's seat of this huge utility vehicle we were approaching.

"*I* will drive," Andy said firmly.

"Aw, Dad," Dopey said. "How'm I ever going to pass the test if you never let me practice?"

"You can practice in the Rambler," Andy said. He opened up the back of his Land Rover, and started putting my bags into it. "That goes for you, too, Suze."

This startled me. "What goes for me, too?"

"You can practice driving in the Rambler." He wagged a finger jokingly in my direction. "But only if there's someone with a valid license in the passenger seat."

I just blinked up at him. "I can't drive," I said.

Dopey let out this big horse laugh. "You can't drive?" He elbowed Sleepy, who was leaning against the side of the truck, his face turned toward the sun. "Hey, Jake, she can't drive!"

"It isn't at all uncommon, Brad," Doc said, "for a native New Yorker to lack a driver's license. Don't you know that New York City boasts the largest mass transit system in North America, serving a population of thirteen point two million people in a four-thousand-square-mile radius fanning out from New York City through Long Island all the way to Connecticut? And that one point seven billion riders take advantage of their extensive fleet of subways, buses, and railroads every year?"

Everybody looked at Doc. Then my mother said carefully, "I never kept a car in the city."

Andy closed the doors to the back of the Land Rover. "Don't worry, Suze," he said. "We'll get you enrolled in a driver's ed course right away. You can take it and catch up to Brad in no time."

I looked at Dopey. Never in a million years had I ever expected that someone would suggest that I needed to catch up to *Brad* in any capacity whatsoever.

But I could see I was in for a lot of surprises. The palm trees had only been the beginning. As we drove to the house, which was a good hour away from the airport—and not a quick hour, either, with me wedged in between Sleepy and Dopey, with Doc in the "way back," perched on top of my luggage, still expounding on the glories of the New York City transportation authority—I began to realize that things were going to be different—very, very different—than I had anticipated, and certainly different from what I was used to.

And not just because I was living on the opposite side of the continent. Not just because everywhere I looked, I saw things I'd never have seen back in New York: roadside stands advertising artichokes or pomegranates, twelve for a dollar; field after field of grapevines, twisting and twisting around wooden arbors; groves of lemon and avocado trees; lush green vegetation I couldn't even identify. And arcing above it all, a sky so blue, so vast, that the hot-air balloon I saw floating through it looked impossibly small—like a button at the bottom of an Olympic-sized swimming pool.

There was the ocean, too, bursting so suddenly into view that at first I didn't recognize it, thinking it was just another field. But then I noticed that this field was sparkling, reflecting the sun, flashing little Morse code SOSs at me. The light was so bright, it was hard to look at without sunglasses. But there it was, the Pacific Ocean . . . huge, stretching almost as wide as the sky, a living, writhing thing, pushing up against a comma-shaped strip of white beach.

Being from New York, my glimpses of ocean—at least the kind with a beach—had been few and far between. I couldn't help gasping when I saw it. And when I gasped, everybody stopped talking—except for Sleepy, who was, of course, asleep.

"What?" my mother asked, alarmed. "What is it?"

"Nothing," I said. I was embarrassed. Obviously, these people were used to seeing the ocean. They were going to think I was some kind of freak that I was getting so excited about it. "Just the ocean."

"Oh," said my mother. "Yes, isn't it beautiful?"

Dopey went, "Good curl on those waves. Might have to hit the beach before dinner."

"Not," his father said, "until you've finished that term paper."

"Aw, Dad!"

This prompted my mother to launch into a long and detailed account of the school to which I was being sent, the same one Sleepy, Dopey, and Doc attended. The school, named after Junipero Serra, some Spanish guy who came over in the 1700s and forced the Native Americans already living here to practice Christianity instead of their own religion, was actually a huge adobe mission that attracted twenty thousand tourists a year, or something.

I wasn't really listening to my mother. My interest in school has always been pretty much zero. The whole reason I hadn't been able to move out here before Christmas was that there had been no space for me at the Mission School, and I'd been forced to wait until second semester started before something opened up. I hadn't minded—I'd gotten to live with my grandmother for a few months, which hadn't been at all bad. My grandmother, besides being a really excellent criminal attorney, is an awesome cook.

I was still sort of distracted by the ocean, which had disappeared behind some hills. I was craning my neck, hoping for another glimpse, when it hit me. I went, "Wait a minute. When was this school built?"

"The eighteenth century," Doc replied. "The mission system, implemented by the Franciscans under the guidelines of the Catholic Church and the Spanish government, was set up not only to Christianize the Native Americans, but also to train them to become successful tradespeople in the new Spanish society. Originally, the mission served as a—"

"Eighteenth century?" I said, leaning forward. I was wedged between Sleepy—whose head had slumped forward until it was resting on my shoulder, enabling me to tell, just by sniffing, that he used Finesse shampoo—and Dopey. Let me tell you, Gina hadn't mentioned a thing about how much room boys take up, which, when they're both nearly six feet tall, and in the two-hundred-pound vicinity, is a lot. "Eighteenth century?"

My mother must have heard the panic in my voice, since she turned in her seat and said soothingly, "Now, Suze, we discussed this. I told you there's a year's waiting list at Robert Louis Stevenson, and you told me you didn't want to go to an all-girls school, so Sacred Heart is out, and Andy's heard some awful stories about drug abuse and gang violence in the public schools around here—"

"Eighteenth century?" I could feel my heart starting to pound hard, as if I'd been running. "That's like *three hundred years old*!"

"I don't get it." We were driving through the town of Carmel-by-the-Sea now, all picturesque cottages—some with thatched roofs, even—and beautiful little restaurants and art galleries. Andy had to drive carefully because the traffic was thick with people in cars with out-of-state licenses, and there weren't any stoplights, something that, for some reason, the natives took pride in. "What's so bad," he wanted to know, "about the eighteenth century?"

My mother said, without any inflection in her voice whatsoever—what I call her bad-news voice, the one she uses on TV to report plane crashes and child murders, "Suze has never been very wild about old buildings."

"Oh," Andy said. "Then I guess she isn't going to like the house."

I gripped the back of his headrest. "Why?" I demanded in a tight voice. "Why am I not going to like the house?"

I saw why, of course, as soon as we pulled in. The house was huge, and impossibly pretty, with Victorian-style turrets and a widow's walk—the whole works. My mom had had it painted blue and white and cream, and it was surrounded by big, shady pine trees, and sprawling, flowering shrubs. Three stories high, constructed entirely from wood, and not the horrible glass-and-steel or terra-cotta stuff the houses around it were made of, it was the loveliest, most tasteful house in the neighborhood.

And I didn't want to set foot in it.

I knew when I'd agreed to move with my mom to California that I'd be in for lots of changes. The roadside artichokes, the lemon groves, the ocean . . . they were nothing, really. The fact was, the biggest change was going to be sharing my mom with other people. In the decade since my father had died, it had been just the two of us. And I have to admit, I sort of liked it like that. In fact, if it hadn't been for the fact that Andy made my mom so obviously happy, I would have put my foot down and said no way to the whole moving thing.

But you couldn't even look at them together—Andy and my mom—and not be able to tell right away that they were completely gaga over each other. And what kind of daughter would I have been if I said no way to that? So I accepted Andy, and I accepted his three sons, and I accepted the fact that I was going to have to leave behind everything I had ever known and loved—my best friend, my grandmother, bagels, SoHo—in order to give my mom the happiness she deserved.

But I hadn't really considered the fact that, for the first time in my life, I was going to have to live in a *house*.

And not just any house, either, but, as Andy proudly told me as he was taking my bags from the car, and thrusting them into his sons' arms, a nineteenth-century converted boardinghouse. Built in 1849, it had apparently had quite a little reputation in its day. Gunfights over card games and women had taken place in the front parlor. You could still see the bullet holes. In fact, Andy had framed one rather than filling it in. It was a bit morbid, he admitted, but interesting, too. He bet we were living in the only house in the

Carmel hills that had a nineteenth-century bullet hole in it.

"Huh," I said. I bet that was true.

My mother kept glancing in my direction as we climbed the many steps to the front porch. I knew she was nervous about what I was going to think. I was kind of irked at her, really, for not warning me. I guess I could understand why she hadn't, though. If she'd told me she had bought a house that was more than a hundred years old, I wouldn't have moved out here. I would have stayed with Grandma until it came time for me to leave for college.

Because my mom's right: I don't like old buildings.

Although I saw, as old buildings went, this one was really something. When you stood on the front porch, you could see all of Carmel beneath you, the village, the valley, the beach, the sea. It was a breathtaking view, one that people would—and had, judging from the fanciness of the houses around ours—pay millions for; one that I shouldn't have resented, not in the least.

And yet, when my mom said, "Come on, Suze. Come see your room," I couldn't help shuddering a little.

The house was as beautiful inside as it was

outside. All shiny maple and cheerful blues and yellows. I recognized my mom's things, and that made me feel a little better. There was the pie-safe she and I had bought once on a weekend trip to Vermont. There were my baby pictures, hanging on the wall in the living room, right alongside Sleepy's, Dopey's, and Doc's. There were my mother's books in the built-in shelves in the den. Her plants, which she'd paid so exorbitant a price to have shipped because she'd been unable to bear parting with them, were everywhere, on wooden stands, hanging in front of the stained-glass windows, perched on top of the newel post at the end of the stairs.

But there were also things I didn't recognize: a sleek white computer sitting on the desk where my mother used to write out checks to pay the bills; a wide-screen TV incongruously tucked into a fireplace in the den, to which shift-sticks were wired for some sort of video game; surfboards leaning up against the wall by the door to the garage; a huge, slobbery dog, who seemed to think I was harboring food in my pockets since he kept thrusting his big wet nose into them.

These all seemed like obtrusively masculine things, foreign things in the life my mother and I had carved out for ourselves. They were going to take some getting used to.

My room was upstairs, just above the roof of the front porch. My mother had been going on nervously for almost the entire trip from the airport about the window seat Andy had installed in the bay window. The bay windows looked out over the same view as the porch, that sweeping vista that incorporated all of the peninsula. It was sweet of them, really, to give me such a nice room, the room with the best view in the whole house.

And when I saw how much trouble they'd gone to, to make the room feel like home to me—or at least to some excessively feminine, phantom girl . . . not *me. I* had never been the glass-topped dressing table, princess phone type—how Andy had put cream-colored wallpaper, dotted with blue forget-me-nots, all along the top of the intricate white wainscoting that lined the walls; how the same wallpaper covered the walls of my own personal adjoining bathroom; how they'd bought me a new bed—a four-poster with a lace canopy, the kind my mother had always wanted for me and had evidently been unable to resist—I felt bad about how I'd acted in the car. I really did. I thought to myself as I walked around the room, *Okay, this isn't so bad. So far you're in the clear.*

*Maybe it'll be all right, maybe no one was ever unhappy in this house, maybe all those people who got shot deserved it. . . .*

Until I turned toward the bay window, and saw that someone was already sitting on the window seat Andy had so lovingly made for me.

Someone who was not related to me, or to Sleepy, Dopey, or Doc.

I turned toward Andy, to see if he'd noticed the intruder. He hadn't, even though he was right there, right in front of his face.

My mother hadn't seen him, either. All she saw was my face. I guess my expression must not have been the most pleasant, since her own fell, and she said with a sad sigh, "Oh, Suze. Not again."

# chapter two

I guess I should explain. I'm not exactly your typical sixteen-year-old girl.

Oh, I *seem* normal enough, I guess. I don't do drugs, or drink, or smoke—well, okay, except for that one time when Sleepy caught me. I don't have anything pierced, except my ears, and only once on each earlobe. I don't have any tattoos. I've never dyed my hair. Except for my boots and leather jacket, I don't wear an excessive amount of black. I don't even wear dark fingernail polish. All in all, I am a pretty normal, everyday, American teenage girl.

Except, of course, for the fact that I can talk to the dead.

I probably shouldn't put it that way. I should probably say that the dead talk to me. I mean, I don't go around initiating these conversations. In fact, I try to avoid the whole thing as much as possible.

It's just that sometimes they won't let me.

The ghosts, I mean.

I don't think I'm crazy. At least, not any crazier than your average sixteen-year-old. I guess I might *seem* crazy to some people. Certainly the majority of kids in my old neighborhood thought I was. Nuts, I mean. I've had the school counselors sicced on me more than once. Sometimes I even think it might be simpler just to *let* them lock me up.

But even on the ninth floor of Bellevue—which is where they lock up the crazy people in New York—I probably wouldn't be safe from the ghosts. They'd find me.

They always do.

I remember my first. I remember it as clearly as any of my other memories of that time, which is to say, not very well, since I was about two years old. I guess I remember it about as well as I remember taking a mouse away from our cat and cradling it in my arms until my horrified mother took it away.

Hey, I was two, okay? I didn't know then that mice were something to be afraid of. Ghosts, either, for that matter. That's why, fourteen years later, neither of them frighten me. Startle me, maybe, sometimes. Annoy me, a lot. But frighten me?

Never.

The ghost, like the mouse, was little, gray, and helpless. To this day, I don't know who she was. I spoke to her, some baby gibberish that she didn't understand. Ghosts can't understand two-year-olds any better than anybody else. She just looked at me sadly from the top of the stairs of our apartment building. I guess I felt sorry for her, the way I had for the mouse, and wanted to help her. Only I didn't know how. So I did what any uncertain two-year-old would do. I ran for my mother.

That was when I learned my first lesson concerning ghosts: only I can see them.

Well, obviously, other people *can* see them. How else would we have haunted houses and ghost stories and *Unsolved Mysteries* and all of that? But there's a difference. Most people who see ghosts only see *one*. I see *all* ghosts.

*All of them.* Anybody. Anybody who has died and for whatever reason is hanging around on Earth instead of going wherever it is he or she is supposed to go, I can see.

And let me tell you, that is *a lot* of ghosts.

I found out the same day that I saw my first ghost that most people—even my own mother—can't see them at all. Neither can anyone else I have ever met. At least, no one who'll admit it.

Which brings us to the second thing I learned about ghosts that day fourteen years ago: It's really better, in the long run, not to mention that you've seen one. Or, as in my case, any.

I'm not saying my mother figured out that it was a ghost I was pointing to and gibbering about that afternoon when I was two. I doubt she knew it. She probably thought I was trying to tell her something about the mouse, which she had confiscated from me earlier that morning. But she looked gamely up the stairs and nodded and said, "Uh-huh. Listen, Suze. What do you want for lunch today? Grilled cheese? Or tuna fish?"

I hadn't exactly expected a reaction similar to the one the mouse had gotten—my mother, who'd been cradling a neighbor's newborn at the time, had let out a glorious shriek at the sight of the mouse in my arms, and had screamed even harder at my proud announcement, "Look, Mommy. Now I've got a baby, too," which I realize now she couldn't have understood, since she didn't get it about the ghost.

But I had expected at least an *acknowledgment* of the thing floating at the top of the stairs. I was given explanations for virtually everything else I encountered on a daily basis, from fire hydrants to electrical outlets. Why not the thing at the top of the stairs?

But as I sat munching my grilled cheese a little later, I realized that the reason my mother had offered no explanation for the gray thing was that she hadn't been able to *see* it. To her, it wasn't there.

At two years old, this didn't seem unreasonable to me. It just seemed, at the time, like another thing that separated children from adults: Children had to eat all their vegetables. Adults did not. Children could ride the merry-go-round in the park. Adults could not. Children could see the gray things. Adults could not.

And even though I was only two years old, I understood that the little gray thing at the top of the stairs was not something to be discussed. Not with anybody. Not ever.

And I never did. I never told anyone about my first ghost, nor did I ever discuss with anyone the hundreds of other ghosts I encountered over the course of the next few years. What was there to discuss, really? I saw them. They spoke to me. For the most part, I didn't understand what they were saying, what they wanted, and they usually went away. End of story.

It probably would have gone on like that indefinitely if my father hadn't suddenly up and died.

Really. Just like that. One minute he was there, cooking and making jokes in the kitchen like he'd always done, and the next day he was gone.

And, people kept assuring me all through the week following his death—which I spent on the stoop in front of our building, waiting for my dad to come home—he was never coming back.

I, of course, didn't believe their assurances. Why should I? My dad, not coming back? Were they nuts? Sure, he might have been dead. I got that part. But he was definitely coming back. Who was going to help me with my math homework? Who was going to wake up early with me on Saturday mornings, and make French toast and watch cartoons? Who was going to teach me to drive, like he'd promised, when I turned sixteen? My dad might have been dead, but I was definitely going to see him again. I saw lots of dead people on a daily basis. Why shouldn't I see my dad?

It turned out I was right. Oh, my dad was dead.

No doubt about that. He'd died of a massive coronary. My mom had his body cremated, and she put his ashes in an antique German beer tankard. You know, that kind with a lid. My dad had always really liked beer. She put the tankard on a shelf, high up, where the cat couldn't knock it over, and sometimes, when she didn't think I was around, I caught her talking to it.

This made me feel really sad. I mean, I guess I couldn't blame her, really. If I didn't know any better, I'd probably have talked to that tankard, too.

But that, you see, was what all those people on my block had been wrong about. My dad was dead, yeah. But I *did* see him again.

In fact, I probably see him more now than I did when he was alive. When he was alive, he had to go to work most days. Now that he's dead, he doesn't have all that much to do. So I see him a lot. Almost too much, in fact. His favorite thing to do is suddenly materialize when I least expect it. It's kind of annoying.

My dad was the one who finally explained it to me. So I guess, in a way, it's a good thing he did die, since I might never have known, otherwise.

Actually, that isn't true. There was a tarot card reader who said something about it once. It was at a school carnival. I only went because Gina didn't want to go alone. I pretty much thought it was a crock, but I went along because that's what best friends do for one another. The woman—Madame Zara, Psychic Medium—read Gina's cards, telling her exactly what she wanted to hear: Oh, you're going to be very successful, you'll be a brain surgeon, you'll marry at thirty, and have three kids, blah, blah, blah. When she was done, I got up to go, but Gina insisted Madame Zara do a reading for me, too.

You can guess what happened. Madame Zara read the cards once, looked confused, and shuffled them up and read them again. Then she looked at me.

"You," she said, "talk to the dead."

This excited Gina. She went, "Oh my God! Oh my God! Really? Suze, did you hear that? You can talk to the dead! You're a psychic medium, too!"

"Not a medium," Madame Zara said. "A *mediator.*"

Gina looked crushed. "A what? What's *that*?"

But I knew. I'd never known what it was called, but I knew what it was. My dad hadn't put it quite that way when he'd explained things, but I got the gist of it, anyway: I am pretty much the contact person for just about anybody who croaks leaving things . . . well, untidy. Then, if I can, I clean up the mess.

That's the only way I can think to explain it. I don't know how I got so lucky—I mean, I am normal in every other respect. Well, almost, anyway. I just have this unfortunate ability to communicate with the dead.

Not *any* dead, either. Only the unhappy dead.

So you can see that my life has really been just a bowl of cherries these past sixteen years.

Imagine, being haunted—literally haunted—by the dead, every single minute of every single day of your life. It is not pleasant. You go down to the deli to get a soda—oops, dead guy on the corner. Somebody shot him. And if you could just make sure the cops get the guy who did it, he can finally rest in peace.

And all you wanted was a soda.

Or you go to the library to check out a book—oops, the ghost of some librarian comes up to you and wants you to tell her nephew how mad she is about what he did with her cats after she kicked the bucket.

And those are just the folks who *know* why they're still sticking around. Half of them don't have any idea why they haven't slipped off into the afterlife like they're supposed to.

Which is irritating because, of course, I'm the schmuck who's supposed to help them get there.

I'm the mediator.

I tell you, it is not a fate I would wish on anybody.

There isn't a whole lot of payoff in the mediation field. It isn't like anyone's ever offered me a salary or anything. Not even *hourly* compensation. Just the occasional warm fuzzies you get when you do a good turn for somebody. Like telling some girl who didn't get to say good-bye to her grandfather before he passed away that he really loves her, and he forgives her for that time she trashed his El Dorado. That kind of thing can warm the heart, it really can.

But for the most part, it's cold pricklies all the way. Besides the hassle—constantly being pestered by folks nobody but you can see—there's the fact that a lot of ghosts are really rude. I mean it. They are royal pains to deal with. These are generally the ones who actually *want* to hang around in this world instead of taking off for the next one. They probably know that based on their behavior in their most recent life, they aren't in for much of a treat in the one they've got coming up. So they just stay here and bug people, slamming doors, knocking over things, making cold spots, groaning. You know what I mean. Your basic poltergeists.

Sometimes, though, they can get rough. I mean, they try to hurt people. On *purpose.* That's when I usually get mad. That's when I usually feel compelled to kick a little ghost butt.

Which was what my mom meant when she said, "Oh, Suze. Not again." When I kick ghost butt, things have a tendency to get a little . . . messy.

Not that I had any intention of messing up my new room. Which is why I turned my back on the ghost sitting on my window seat and said, "Never mind, Mom. Everything's fine. The room is great. Thanks so much."

I could tell she didn't believe me. It's hard to fake out my mom. I know she suspects there's something up with me. She just can't figure out what it is. Which is probably a good thing because it would shake up the world as she knows it in too major a way. I mean, she's a television news reporter. She only believes what she can see. And she can't see ghosts.

I can't tell you how much I wish I could be like her.

"Well," she said, "I'm glad you like it. I was sort of worried. I mean, I know how you get about . . . well, old places."

Old places are the worst for me because the older a building is, the more chance there is that someone has died in it, and that he or she is still hanging around there looking for justice or waiting to deliver some final message to someone. Let me tell you, this led to some pretty interesting results back when my mom and I used to go apartment hunting in the city. We would walk into these seemingly perfect apartments, and I'd be like, "Nuh-uh. No way," for no reason that I could actually explain. It's really a wonder my mom never just packed me off to boarding school.

"Really, Mom," I said. "It's great. I love it."

Andy, hearing this, hustled around the room all excitedly, showing me the clap-on, clap-off lights (oh, boy) and various other gadgets he'd installed. I followed him around, expressing my delight, being careful not to look in the ghost's direction. It really was sweet, how much Andy wanted me to be happy. And I was determined, because he wanted it so much, to *be* happy. At least as happy as it's possible for someone like me to be.

After a while, Andy ran out of stuff to show me, and went away to start the barbecue, since in honor of my arrival, we were having surf and turf for dinner. Sleepy and Dopey took off to "hit some waves" before we ate, and Doc, muttering mysteriously about an "experiment" he'd been working on, drifted off to another part of the house, leaving me alone with my mother . . . well, sort of.

"Is it *really* all right, Suze?" my mom wanted to know. "I know it's a big change. I know it's asking a lot of you—"

I took off my leather jacket. I don't know if I've mentioned this, but it was pretty hot out for January. Like seventy. I'd nearly roasted in the car. "It's fine, Mom," I said. "Really."

"I mean, asking you to leave Grandma, and Gina, and New York. It's selfish of me, I know. I know things haven't been . . . well, easy for you. Especially since Daddy died."

My mother likes to think that the reason I'm not like the traditional teenage girl she was when she was my age—she was a cheerleader, and homecoming queen, and had lots of boyfriends and stuff—is that I lost my father at such an early age. She blames his death for everything, from the fact that I have no friends—with the exception of Gina—to the fact that I sometimes engage in extremely weird behavior.

And I suppose some of the stuff I've done in the past would seem pretty weird to someone who didn't know why I was doing it, or couldn't see who I was doing it for. I have certainly been caught any number of times in places I wasn't supposed to be. I've been brought home by the police a few times, accused of trespassing or vandalism or breaking and entering.

And while I've never actually been convicted of anything, I've spent any number of hours in my mother's therapist's office, being assured that this tendency I have to talk to myself is perfectly normal, but that my propensity to talk to people *who aren't there* probably isn't.

Ditto my dislike of any building not constructed in the past five years.

Ditto the amount of time I spend in graveyards, churches, temples, mosques, other people's (locked) apartments or houses, and school grounds after hours.

I suppose Andy's boys must have overheard something about this, and that's where the whole gang thing came from. But like I said, I've never actually served time for anything I've done.

And that two-week suspension in the eighth grade isn't even reflected on my permanent record.

So maybe it wasn't so unusual for my mother to be sitting there on my bed, talking about "fresh starts" and all of that. It was kind of weird that she was doing it while this ghost was sitting a few feet away, watching us. But whatever. She seemed to have a need to talk about how things were going to be much better for me out here on the West Coast.

And if that's what she wanted, I was going to do my best to make sure she got it. I had already resolved not to do anything out here that was going to end up getting me arrested, so that was a start, anyway.

"Well," my mom said, running out of steam after her you-won't-make-friends-unless-you-project-a-friendly-demeanor speech. "I guess if you don't want help unpacking, I'll go see how Andy is doing with dinner."

Andy, in addition to being able to build just about anything, was also an excellent cook, something my mother most definitely was not.

I said, "Yeah, Mom, you go do that. I'll just get settled in here, and I'll be down in a minute."

My mom nodded and got up—but she wasn't about to let me escape that easily. Just as she was about to go out the door, she turned around and said, her blue eyes all filled with tears, "I just want you to be happy, Susie. That's all I've ever wanted. Do you think you can be happy here?"

I gave her a hug. I'm as tall as she is, in my ankle boots. "Sure, Mom," I said. "Sure, I'll be happy here. I feel at home already."

"Really?" My mom was sniffling. "You swear?"

"I do." And I wasn't lying, either. I mean, there'd been ghosts in my bedroom back in Brooklyn all the time, too.

She went away, and I shut the door quietly behind her. I waited until I couldn't hear her heels on the stairs anymore, and then I turned around.

"All right," I said, to the presence on the window seat. "Who the hell are you?"

# chapter three

To say that the guy looked *surprised* to be addressed in this manner would have been a massive understatement. He didn't just look surprised. He actually looked over his shoulder, to see if it was really him I was talking to.

But of course, the only thing behind him was the window, and through it, that incredible view of Carmel Bay. So then he turned back to look at me, and must have seen that my gaze was fastened directly on his face, since he breathed, *"Nombre de Dios,"* in a manner that would have had Gina, who has a thing for Latino guys, swooning.

"It's no use calling on your higher power," I

informed him, as I swung the pink-tasseled chair to my new dressing table around, and straddled it. "In case you haven't noticed, He isn't paying a whole lot of attention to you. Otherwise, He wouldn't have left you here to fester for—" I took in his outfit, which looked a lot like something they'd have worn on *The Wild, Wild West.* "What is it, a hundred and fifty years? Has it really been that long since you croaked?"

He stared at me with eyes that were as black and liquid as ink. "What is . . . croaked?" he asked, in a voice that sounded rusty from disuse.

I rolled my eyes. "Kicked the bucket," I translated. "Checked out. Popped off. Bit the dust." When I saw from his perplexed expression that he still didn't understand, I said, with some exasperation, *"Died."*

"Oh," he said. "Died." But instead of answering my question, he shook his head. "I don't understand," he said, in tones of wonder. "I don't understand how it is that you can see me. All these years, no one has ever—"

"Yeah," I said, cutting him off. I hear this kind of thing a lot, you understand. "Well, listen, the times, you know, they are a-changin'. So what's your glitch?"

He blinked at me with those big dark eyes. His

eyelashes were longer than mine. It isn't often I run into a ghost who also happens to be a hottie, but this guy . . . boy, he must have been something back when he was alive because here he was dead and I was already trying to catch a peek at what was going on beneath the white shirt he was wearing very much open at the throat, exposing quite a bit of his chest, and some of his stomach, too. Do ghosts have six-packs? This was not something I had ever had occasion—or a desire—to explore before.

Not that I was about to let myself get distracted by that kind of thing now. I'm a professional, after all.

"Glitch?" he echoed. Even his voice was liquid, his English as flat and unaccented as I fancied my own was, slight Brooklyn blurring of my t's aside. He clearly had some Spaniard in him, as his *Dios* and his coloring indicated, but he was as American as I was—or as American as someone who was born before California became a state *could* be.

"Yeah." I cleared my throat. He had turned a little and put a boot up onto the pale blue cushion that covered the window seat, and I had seen definitive proof that yes, ghosts could indeed have six-packs. His abdominal muscles were deeply ridged, and covered with a light dusting of silky black hair.

I swallowed. Hard.

"Glitch," I said. "Problem. Why are you still here?" He looked at me, his expression blank, but interested. I elaborated. *"Why haven't you gone to the other side?"*

He shook his head. Have I mentioned that his hair was short and dark and sort of crisp-looking, like if you touched it, it would be really, really thick? "I don't know what you mean."

I was getting sort of warm, but I had already taken off my leather jacket, so I didn't know what to do about it. I couldn't very well take off anything else with him sitting there watching me. This realization might have contributed to my suddenly very foul mood.

"What do you mean, you don't know what I mean?" I snapped, pushing some hair away from my eyes. "You're *dead.* You don't belong here. You're supposed to be off doing whatever it is that happens to people after they're dead. Rejoicing in heaven, or burning in hell, or being reincarnated, or ascending another plane of consciousness, or whatever. You're not supposed to be just . . . well, just *hanging around.*"

He looked at me thoughtfully, balancing his

elbow on his uplifted knee, his arm sort of dangling. "And what if I happen to like just *hanging around*?" he wanted to know.

I wasn't sure, but I had a feeling he was making fun of me. And I don't like being made fun of. I really don't. People back in Brooklyn used to do it all the time—well, until I learned how effectively a fist connecting with their nose could shut them up.

I wasn't ready to hit this guy—not yet. But I was close. I mean, I'd just traveled a gazillion miles for what seemed like days in order to live with a bunch of stupid boys; I still had to unpack; I had already practically made my mother cry; and then I find a ghost in my bedroom. Can you blame me for being . . . well, short with him?

"Look," I said, standing up fast, and swinging my leg around the back of the chair. "You can do all the hanging around you want, *amigo*. Slack away. I don't really care. But you can't do it here."

"Jesse," he said, not moving.

"What?"

"You called me *amigo*. I thought you might like to know I have a name. It's Jesse."

I nodded. "Right. That figures. Well, fine. Jesse, then. You can't stay here, Jesse."

"And you?" Jesse was smiling at me now. He

had a nice face. A good face. The kind of face that, back in my old high school, would have gotten him elected prom king in no time flat. The kind of face Gina would have cut out of a magazine and taped to her bedroom wall.

Not that he was pretty. Not at all. Dangerous was how he looked. Mighty dangerous.

"And me, what?" I knew I was being rude. I didn't care.

"What is your name?"

I glared at him. "Look. Just tell me what you want, and get out. I'm hot, and I want to change clothes. I don't have time for—"

He interrupted, as amiably as if he hadn't heard me talking at all, "That woman—your mother—called you Susie." His black eyes were bright on me. "Short for Susan?"

"Susannah," I said, correcting him automatically. "As in, 'Don't you cry for me.'"

He smiled. "I know the song."

"Yeah. It was probably in the top forty the year you were born, huh?"

He just kept on smiling. "So this is your room now, is it, Susannah?"

"Yeah," I said. "Yeah, this is my room now. So you're going to have clear out."

"*I'm* going to have to clear out?" He raised one

black eyebrow. "This has been my home for a century and a half. Why do *I* have to leave it?"

"Because." I was getting really mad. Mostly because I was so hot, and I wanted to open a window, but the windows were behind him, and I didn't want to get that close to him. "This is *my* room. I'm not sharing it with some dead cowboy."

That got to him. He slammed his foot back down on the floor—hard—and stood up. I instantly wished I hadn't said anything. He was tall, way taller than me, and in my ankle boots I'm five eight.

"I am *not* a cowboy," he informed me angrily. He added something in Spanish in an undertone, but since I had always taken French, I had no idea what he was saying. At the same time, the antique mirror hanging over my new dressing table started to wobble dangerously on the hook that held it to the wall. This was not due, I knew, to a California earthquake, but to the agitation of the ghost in front of me, whose psychic abilities were obviously of a kinetic bent.

That's the thing about ghosts: They're so touchy! The slightest thing can set them off.

"Whoa," I said, holding up both my hands, palms outward. "Down. Down, boy."

"My family," Jesse raged, wagging a finger in my face, "worked like slaves to make something of themselves in this country, but never, never as a *vaquero*—"

"Hey," I said. And that's when I made my big mistake. I reached out, not liking the finger he was jabbing at me, and grabbed it, hard, yanking on his hand and pulling him toward me so I could be sure he heard me as I hissed, "Stop with the mirror already. And stop shoving your finger in my face. Do it again, and I'll break it."

I flung his hand away, and saw, with satisfaction, that the mirror had stopped shaking. But then I happened to glance at his face.

Ghosts don't have blood. How can they? They aren't alive. But I swear, at that moment, all the color drained from Jesse's face, as if every ounce of blood that had once been there had evaporated just at that moment.

Not being alive, and not possessing blood, it follows that ghosts aren't made of matter, either. So it didn't make sense that I had been able to grab his finger. My hand should have passed right through him. Right?

Wrong. That's how it works for most people. But not for people like me. Not for the mediators. We can see ghosts, we can talk to ghosts, and, if necessary, we can kick a ghost's butt.

But this isn't something I like to go around advertising. I try to avoid touching them—touching anybody, really—as much as possible. If all attempts at mediation have failed, and I have to use a little physical coercion on a recalcitrant spirit, I generally prefer him or her not to know beforehand that I am capable of doing so. Sneak attacks are always advisable when dealing with members of the underworld, who are notoriously dirty fighters.

Jesse, looking down at his finger as if I'd burned a hole through it, seemed perfectly incapable of saying anything. It was probably the first time he'd been touched by anyone in a century and a half. That kind of thing can blow a guy's mind. Especially a dead guy.

I took advantage of his astonishment, and said, in my sternest, most no-nonsense tone, "Now, look, Jesse. This is my room, understand? You can't stay here. You've either got to let me help you get to where you're supposed to go, or you're going to have to find some other house to haunt. I'm sorry, but that's the way it is."

Jesse looked up from his finger, his expression still one of utter disbelief. "Who *are* you?" he asked softly. "What kind of . . . girl are you?"

He hesitated so long before he said the word *girl* that it was clear he wasn't at all certain it was appropriate in my case. This kind of bugged me. I mean, I may not have been the most popular girl in school, but no one ever denied I was an actual girl. Truck drivers honk at me at crosswalks now and then, and not because they want me to get out of the way. Construction workers sometimes holler rude things at me, especially when I wear my leather miniskirt. I am not unattractive, or mannish in any way. Sure, I'd just threatened to break his finger off, but that didn't mean I wasn't a *girl,* for God's sake!

"I'll tell you what kind of girl I'm not," I said crankily. "I am *not* the kind of girl who's looking to share her room with a member of the opposite sex. Understand me? So either you move out, or I force you out. It's entirely up to you. I'll give you some time to think about it. But when I get back here, Jesse, I want you gone."

I turned around and left.

I had to. I don't usually lose arguments with ghosts, but I had a feeling I was losing that one, and badly. I shouldn't have been so short with him, and I shouldn't have been rude. I don't know what came over me, I really don't. I just . . .

I guess I just wasn't expecting to find the ghost

of such a cute guy in my bedroom, is all.

*God,* I thought, as I stormed down the hall. *What am I going to do if he doesn't leave? I won't be able to change clothes in my own room!*

*Give him a little time,* a voice inside my head went. It was a voice I'd very carefully avoided telling my mom's therapist about.

*Give him a little time. He'll come around. They always do.*

Well, most of the time, anyway.

# chapter *four*

Dinner at the Ackerman household was pretty much like dinner in any other large household I had ever known: Everybody talked at once—except of course for Sleepy, who only spoke when asked a direct question—and nobody wanted to clear the table afterward. I made a mental note to call Gina and tell her she'd been wrong. There really was no advantage, that I could see, in having brothers: They chewed with their mouths open, and ate every single Poppin' Fresh bread roll before I'd even had one.

After dinner, I decided it would be wise to avoid my room, and give Jesse plenty of time to make up his mind about whether he was leaving with or without his teeth. I'm not a big fan of violence, but it's an unfortunate by-product of my profession. Sometimes, the only way you can make someone listen is with your fist. This is not a technique espoused, I know, by the diagnostic manuals on most therapists' shelves.

Then again, nobody ever said I was a therapist.

The problem with my plan, of course, was that it was Saturday night. I'd forgotten what day it was in all the stress of the move. Back home on a Saturday night, I'd probably have gone out with Gina, taken the subway to the Village and gone to see a movie, or just hung around Joe's Pizza watching people walk by. Hey, I may be a big-city girl, but that doesn't mean my life there was glamorous by any means. I have never even been asked out by a boy, unless you count that time in the fifth grade when Daniel Bogue asked me to skate with him during a couples-only song at Rockefeller Center's ice rink.

And then I'd embarrassed myself by falling flat on my face.

My mom, however, was all anxious for me to throw myself into the social scene of Carmel. As soon as the dishwasher was loaded, she was like, "Brad, what are you doing tonight? Are there any parties, or anything? Maybe you could take Suze and introduce her to some people."

Dopey, who was mixing himself a protein shake—apparently, the two dozen jumbo shrimps and massive shell steak he'd consumed at dinner hadn't been filling enough—went, "Yeah, maybe I could, if Jake wasn't working tonight."

Sleepy, roused by the mention of his name, squinted down at his watch and said, "Damn," picked up his jean jacket, and left the house.

Doc looked at the clock and made a *tsk-tsk*ing noise. "Late again. He's going to get himself fired if he doesn't watch it."

Sleepy had a job? This was news to me, so I asked, "Where's he work?"

"Peninsula Pizza." Doc was performing some sort of bizarre experiment that involved the dog and my mother's treadmill. The dog, who was huge—a cross between a St. Bernard and a bear, I think—was sitting very patiently on the floor while Doc attached electrodes to small patches of the dog's skin he'd shaved free of fur. The strangest thing was that nobody seemed to mind this, least of all the dog.

"Slee—I mean, Jake works in a pizza place?"

Andy, scouring a baking dish in the sink, said, "He delivers for them. Brings home a bundle in tips."

"He's saving up," Dopey informed me, a thick white milkshake mustache on his upper lip, "for a Camaro."

"Huh," I said.

"You guys want me to drop you anywhere," Andy offered generously, "I'd be happy to. Whaddya say, Brad? Want to show Suze the action down at the mall?"

"Nah," Dopey said, wiping his mouth with the sleeve of his sweatshirt. "Everybody's still up in Tahoe for the break. Next weekend, maybe."

I nearly collapsed with relief. The word *mall* always filled me with a sort of horror, a horror that had nothing to do with the undead. They don't have malls in New York City, but Gina used to love to take the PATH train to this one in New Jersey. Usually after about an hour, I'd develop sensory overload, and have to sit down in the This Can't Be Yogurt and sip an herbal tea until I calmed down.

And I have to admit, I wasn't that thrilled with the idea of anybody "dropping" me somewhere. My God, what was *wrong* with this place? I could see how, given the San Andreas fault, subways might not be such a great idea, but why hadn't anybody established a decent bus system?

"I know," Dopey said, slamming his empty glass down. "I'll play you a few games of Cool Boarders, Suze."

I blinked at him. "You'll what?"

"I'll play you in Cool Boarders." When my expression remained blank, Dopey said, "You never heard of Cool Boarders? Come on."

He led me toward the wide-screen TV in the den. Cool Boarders, it turned out, was a video game. Each player got assigned a snowboarder, and then you raced each other down various slopes using a joystick to control how fast your boarder went and what kind of fancy moves she might make.

I beat Dopey at it eight times before he finally said, "Let's watch a movie instead."

Sensing that I had probably erred in some way—I guess I should have let the poor boy win at least once—I tried to make amends by volunteering to supply the popcorn, and went into the kitchen.

It was only then that a wave of tiredness hit me. There is a three-hour time difference between New York and California, so even though it was only nine o'clock, I was as tired as if it were midnight. Andy and my mom had retired to the massive master bedroom, but they had left the door to it wide open, I guess so that we wouldn't get any wrong ideas about what they were doing in there. Andy was reading a spy novel, and my mother was watching a made-for-TV movie.

This, I was sure, was strictly for the benefit of us kids; most other Saturday nights I bet they'd have closed that door, or at least have gone out with Andy's friends or my mom's new colleagues at the TV station in Monterey where she'd been hired. They were obviously trying to establish some sort of domestic pattern to make us kids feel secure. You had to give them snaps for doing their best.

I wondered, as I stood there, waiting for the popcorn to pop, what my dad thought of all this. He hadn't been too enthused about Mom's remarrying, even though, as I've said, Andy is a pretty great guy. He'd been even less enthused about my moving out to the West Coast.

"How," he'd wanted to know, when I told him, "am I going to pop in on you when you're living three thousand miles away?"

"The point, Dad," I'd said to him, "is that you aren't supposed to be popping in on me. You're supposed to be dead, remember? You're supposed to be doing whatever it is dead people do, not spying on me and Mom."

He'd looked sort of hurt by that. "I'm not spying," he'd said. "I'm just checking up. To make sure you're happy, and all of that."

"Well, I am," I'd assured him. "I'm very happy, and so is Mom."

I'd been lying, of course. Not about Mom, but about me. I'd been a nervous wreck at the prospect of moving. Even now, I wasn't really sure it was going to work out. This thing with Jesse . . . I mean, where was my dad, anyway? Why wasn't he upstairs kicking that guy's butt? Jesse was, after all, a boy, and he was in my bedroom, and fathers are supposed to hate that kind of thing. . . .

But that's the thing about ghosts. They are never around when you actually need them. Even if they happen to be your dad.

I guess I must have zoned out for a little while because next thing I knew, the microwave was dinging. I took the popcorn out and opened the bag. I was pouring it into a big wooden bowl when my mom came into the kitchen and switched on the overhead light.

"Hi, honey," she said. Then she looked at me. "Are you all right, Susie?"

"Sure, Mom," I said. I shoveled some popcorn

into my mouth. "Dope—I mean, *Brad* and I are gonna watch a movie."

"Are you sure?" My mother was peering at me curiously. "Are you sure you're all right?"

"Yeah, I'm fine. Just tired, is all."

She looked relieved. "Oh, yes. Well, I expected you'd have a bit of jet lag. But . . . well, it's just that you looked so upset when you first walked into your room upstairs. I know the canopy bed was a bit much, but I couldn't resist."

I chewed. I was totally used to this kind of thing. "The bed's fine, Mom," I said. "The room's fine, too."

"I'm so glad," my mom said, pushing a strand of hair from my eyes. "I'm so glad you like it, Suze."

My mother looked so relieved, I sort of felt sorry for her, in a way. I mean, she's a nice lady and doesn't deserve to have a mediator for a daughter. I know I've always been a bit of a disappointment to her. When I turned fourteen, she got me my own phone line, thinking so many boys would be calling me, her friends would never be able to get through. You can imagine how disappointed she was when nobody except Gina ever called me on my private line, and then it was usually only to tell me about the dates *she'd* been on. Like I said, the boys in my neighborhood were never much interested in asking *me* out.

My poor mom. She always wanted a nice, normal teenage daughter. Instead, she got me.

"Honey," she said. "Don't you want to change? You've been wearing those same clothes since six o'clock this morning, haven't you?"

She asked me this right as Doc was coming in to get more glue for his electrodes. Not that I was going to say anything like, *Well, to tell you the truth, Mom, I'd like to change, but I'm not real excited about doing it in front of the ghost of the dead cowboy that's living in my room.*

Instead, I shrugged and said with elaborate casualness, "Yeah, well, I'm gonna change in a bit."

"Are you sure you don't want help unpacking? I feel terrible. I should have—"

"No, I don't need any help. I'll unpack in a bit." I watched Doc forage through a drawer. "I better go," I said. "I don't want to miss the beginning of the movie."

Of course, in the end, I missed the beginning middle, and end of the movie. I fell asleep on the couch, and didn't wake up until Andy shook my shoulder a little after eleven.

"Up and at 'em, kiddo," he said. "I think it's time to admit you've gone down for the count. Don't worry. Brad won't tell anybody."

I got up groggily, and made my way up to my room. I headed straight for the windows, which I yanked open. To my relief there was no Jesse to block the way. *Yes.* I've still got it.

I grabbed my duffel bag and went into the bathroom where I showered and, just to be on the safe side—I didn't know for sure whether or not Jesse had gotten the message and vamoosed—changed into my pajamas. When I came out of the bathroom, I was a little more awake. I looked around, feeling the cool breeze seeping in, smelling the salt in the air. Unlike back in Brooklyn, where our ears were under constant assault by sirens and car alarms, it was quiet in the hills, the only sound the occasional hoot of an owl.

I found, rather to my surprise, that I was alone. Really alone. A ghost-free zone. Exactly what I'd always wanted.

I got into bed and clapped my hands, dousing the lights. Then I snuggled deep beneath my crisp new sheets.

Just before I fell asleep again, I thought I heard something besides the owl. It sounded like someone singing the words *Oh, Susannah, now don't you cry for me, 'cause I come from Alabama with this banjo on my knee.*

But that, I'm sure, was just my imagination.

# chapter *five*

The Junipero Serra Catholic Academy, grades K–12, had been made coeducational in the 1980s, and had, much to my relief, recently dropped its strict uniform policy. The uniforms had been royal blue and white, not my best colors. Fortunately, the uniforms had been so unpopular that they, like the boys-only rule, had been abandoned, and though the pupils still couldn't wear jeans, they could wear just about anything else they wanted. Since all I wanted was to wear my extensive collection of designer clothing—purchased at various outlet stores in New Jersey with Gina as my fashion coordinator—this suited me fine.

The Catholic thing, though, was going to be a problem. Not really a problem so much as an inconvenience. You see, my mother never really bothered to raise me in any particular religion. My father was a nonpracticing Jew, my mother Christian. Religion had never played an important part in either of my parents' lives, and, needless to say, it had only served to confuse me. I mean, you would think I'd have a better grasp on religion than anybody, but the truth is, I haven't the slightest idea what happens to the ghosts I send off to wherever it is they're supposed to go after they die. All I know is, once I send them there, they do not come back. Not ever. The end.

So when my mother and I showed up at the Mission School's administrative office the Monday after my arrival in sunny California, I was more than a little taken aback to be confronted with a six-foot Jesus hanging on a crucifix behind the secretary's desk.

I shouldn't have been surprised, though. My mom had pointed out the school from my room on Sunday morning as she helped me to unpack. "See that big red dome?" she'd said. "That's the Mission. The dome covers the chapel."

Doc happened to be hanging around—I'd noticed he did that a lot—and he launched into another one of his descriptions, this time of the Franciscans, who were members of a Roman Catholic religious order that followed the rule of St. Francis, approved in 1209. Father Junipero Serra, a Franciscan monk, was, according to Doc, a tragically misunderstood historical figure. A controversial hero in the Catholic church, he had been considered for sainthood at one time, but, Doc explained, Native Americans questioned this move as "a general endorsement of the exploitative colonization tactics of the Spanish. Though Junipero Serra was known to have argued on behalf of the property rights and economic entitlement of converted Native Americans, he consistently advocated against their right to self-governance, and was a staunch supporter of corporal punishment, appealing to the Spanish government for the right to flog Indians."

When Doc had finished this particular lecture, I just looked at him and went, "Photographic memory much?"

He looked embarrassed. "Well," he said. "It's good to know the history of the place where you're living."

I filed this away for future reference. Doc might be just the person I needed if Jesse showed up again.

Now, standing in the cool office of the ancient building Junipero Serra had constructed for the betterment of the natives in the area, I wondered how many ghosts I was going to encounter. That Serra guy had to have a bunch of Native Americans mad at him—particularly considering that corporal punishment thing—and I hadn't any doubt I was going to encounter all of them.

And yet, when my mom and I walked through the school's wide front archway into the courtyard around which the Mission had been constructed, I didn't see a single person who looked as if he or she didn't belong there. There were a few tourists snapping pictures of the impressive fountain, a gardener working diligently at the base of a palm tree—even at my new school there were palm trees—a priest walking in silent contemplation down the airy breezeway. It was a beautiful, restful place—especially for a building that was so old and had to have seen so much death.

I couldn't understand it. Where were all the ghosts?

Maybe they were afraid to hang around the place. *I* was a little afraid, looking up at that crucifix. I mean, I've got nothing against religious art, but was it really necessary to portray the crucifixion so realistically, with so many scabs and all?

Apparently, I was not alone in thinking so, since a boy who was slumped on a couch across from the one where my mom and I had been instructed to wait noticed the direction of my gaze and said, "He's supposed to weep tears of blood if any girl ever graduates from here a virgin."

I couldn't help letting out a little bark of laughter. My mother glared at me. The secretary, a plump middle-aged woman who looked as if something like that ought to have offended her deeply, only rolled her eyes, and said tiredly, "Oh, Adam."

Adam, a good-looking boy about my age, looked at me with a perfectly serious face. "It's true," he said gravely. "It happened last year. My sister." He dropped his voice conspiratorially. "She's adopted."

I laughed again, and my mother frowned at me. She had spent most of yesterday explaining to me that it had been really, really hard to convince the school to take me, especially since she couldn't produce any proof that I'd ever been baptized. In the end, they'd only let me in because of Andy, since all three of his boys went there. I imagine a sizable donation had also played a part in my admittance, but my mother wouldn't tell me that. All she said was that I had better behave myself, and not hurl anything out of any windows—even though I reminded her that that particular incident hadn't been my fault. I'd been fighting with a particularly violent young ghost who'd refused to quit haunting the girls' locker room at my old school. Throwing him through that window had certainly gotten his attention, and convinced him to trod the path of righteousness ever after.

Of course, I'd told my mother that I'd been practicing my tennis swing indoors, and the racket had slipped from my hands—an especially unbelievable story, since a racket was never found.

It was as I was reliving this painful memory that a heavy wooden door opened, and a priest came out and said, "Mrs. Ackerman, what a pleasure to see you again. And this must be Susannah Simon. Come in, won't you?" He ushered us into his office, then paused, and said to the boy on the couch, "Oh, no, Mr. McTavish. Not on the first day of a brand-new semester."

Adam shrugged. "What can I say? The broad hates me."

"Kindly do not refer to Sister Ernestine as a broad, Mr. McTavish. I will see to you in a moment, after I have spoken with these ladies."

We went in, and the principal, Father Dominic—that was his name—sat and chatted with us for a while, asking me how I liked California so far. I said I liked it fine, especially the ocean. We had spent most of the day before at the beach, after I'd finished unpacking. I had found my sunglasses, and even though it was too cold to swim, I had a great time just lying on a blanket on the beach, watching the waves. They were huge, bigger than on *Baywatch,* and Doc spent most of the afternoon explaining to me why that was. I forget now, since I was so drugged by the sun, I was hardly even listening. I found that I loved the beach, the smell of it, the seaweed that washed up on shore, the feel of the cool sand between my toes, the taste of salt on my skin when I got home. Carmel might not have had a Bagel Bob's, but Manhattan sure didn't have no beach.

Father Dominic expressed his sincere hope that I'd be happy at the Mission Academy, and went on to explain that even though I wasn't Catholic, I shouldn't feel unwelcome at Mass. There were, of course, Holy Days of Obligation, when the Catholic students would be required to leave their lessons behind and go to church. I could either join them, or stay behind in the empty classroom, whatever I chose.

I thought this was kind of funny, for some reason, but I managed to keep from laughing. Father Dominic was old, but what you'd probably call spry, and he struck me as sort of handsome in his white collar and black robes—I mean, handsome for a sixty-year-old. He had white hair, and very blue eyes, and well-maintained fingernails. I don't know many priests, but I thought this one might be all right—especially since he hadn't come down hard on the boy in the outer office who'd called that nun a broad.

After Father Dominic had described the various offenses I could get expelled for—skipping class too many times, dealing drugs on campus, the usual stuff—he asked me if I had any questions. I didn't. Then he asked my mother if she had any questions. She didn't. So then Father Dominic stood up and said, "Fine then. I'll say good-bye to you, Mrs. Ackerman, and walk Susannah to her first class. All right, Susannah?"

I thought it was kind of weird that the principal, who probably had a lot to do, was taking time out to walk me to my first class, but I didn't say anything about it. I just picked up my coat—a black wool trench by Esprit, *très chic* (my mom wouldn't let me wear leather my first day of school)—and waited while he and my mother shook hands. My mom kissed me good-bye, and reminded me to find Sleepy at 3:00, since he was in charge of driving me home—only she didn't call him Sleepy. Once again, a woeful lack of public transportation meant that I had to bum rides to and from school with my stepbrothers.

Then she was gone, and Father Dominic was walking me across the courtyard after having instructed Adam to wait for him.

"No prob, *padre*," was Adam's response. He leered at me behind the father's back. It isn't often I get leered at by boys my own age. I hoped he was in my class. My mother's wishes for my social life just might be realized at last.

As we walked, Father Dominic explained a little about the building—or buildings, I should say, since that's what they were. A series of thick-walled adobe structures were connected by low-ceilinged breezeways, in the middle of which existed the beautiful courtyard that came complete with palm trees, bubbling fountain, and a bronze statue of Father Serra with these women—your stereotypical Indian squaws, complete with papooses strapped to their backs—kneeling at his feet. On the other side of the breezeway were stone benches for people to sit on while they enjoyed solitary contemplation of the courtyard's splendor, the doors to the classrooms and steel lockers were built right into the adobe wall. One of those lockers, Father Dominic explained to me, was mine. He had the combination with him. Did I want to put away my coat?

I had been surprised when I'd wakened Sunday morning to find myself shivering in my bed. I'd had to stumble out from beneath the sheets and slam my windows shut. A thick fog, I saw with dismay, had enshrouded the valley, obscuring my view of the bay. I thought for sure some horrible tropical storm had rolled in, but Doc had explained to me, quite patiently, that morning fog was typical in the Northwest, and that the *Pacífico*—Spanish for passive—was so named because of its relative lack of storms. The fog, Doc had assured me, would burn off by noon, and it would then be just as hot as it had been the day before.

And he'd been right. By the time I returned home from the beach, sunburned and happy, my room had become an oven again, and I'd pried the windows back open—only to find that they'd been gently shut again when I woke up this morning, which I thought was sweet of my mom, looking out for me like that.

At least, I *hope* it was my mom. Now that I think about it . . . but no, I hadn't seen Jesse since that first day I'd moved in. It had definitely been my mom who'd shut my windows.

Anyway, when I'd walked outside to get into Mom's car, I'd found that it was freezing out again, and that was why I was wearing the wool coat.

Father Dominic told me that my locker was number 273, and he seemed content to let me find it myself, strolling behind me with his eyes on the breezeway's rafters, in which, much to his professed delight, families of swallows nested every year. He was apparently quite fond of birds—of all animals, actually, since one of the questions he'd asked me was how was I getting along with Max, the Ackermans' dog—and openly scoffed at Andy's repeated assurances that the timber in the breezeways was going to have to be replaced thanks to the swallows and their refuse.

268, 269, 270. I strolled down the open corridor, watching the numbers on the beige locker doors. Unlike the ones in my school back in Brooklyn, these lockers were not graffitied, or dented, or plastered with stickers from heavy metal bands. I guess students on the West Coast took more pride in their school's appearance than us Yankees.

271, 272. I stumbled to a halt.

In front of locker number 273 stood a ghost.

It wasn't Jesse, either. It was a girl, dressed very much like I was, only with long blonde hair, instead of brown, like mine. She also had an extremely unpleasant look on her face.

"What," she said to me, "are *you* looking at?" Then, speaking to someone behind me, she demanded, "*This* is who they let in to take my place? I am *so* sure."

Okay, I admit it. I freaked out. I spun around, and found myself gaping up at Father Dominic, who was squinting down at me curiously.

"Ah," he said, when he saw my face. "I thought so."

# chapter six

I looked from Father Dominic to the ghost girl, and back again. Finally, I managed to blurt out, "You can *see* her?"

He nodded. "Yes. I suspected when I first heard your mother speak about you—and your . . . *problems* at your old school—that you might be one of us, Susannah. But I couldn't be sure, of course, so I didn't say anything. Although the name Simon, I'm sure you're aware, is from the Hebrew word meaning "intent listener," which, as a fellow mediator, you of course would be. . . ."

I barely heard him. I couldn't get over the fact that finally, after all these years, I'd met another mediator.

"So *that's* why there aren't any Indian spirits around here!" I practically yelled. "*You* took care of them. Jeez, I was *wondering* what happened to them all. I expected to find hundreds—"

Father Dominic bowed his head modestly and said, "Well, there weren't hundreds, exactly, but when I first arrived, there were quite a few. But it was nothing, really. I was only doing my duty, after all, making use of the heavenly gift I received from God."

I made a face. "Is *that* who's responsible for it?"

"But of course ours is a gift from God." Father Dominic looked down at me with that special kind of pity the faithful always bestow upon us poor, pathetic creatures who have doubts. "Where else do you think it could come from?"

"I don't know. I've always kind of wanted to have a word with the guy in charge, you know? Because, given a choice, I'd much rather not have been blessed with this particular gift."

Father Dominic looked surprised. "But why ever not, Susannah?"

"All it does is get me into trouble. Do you have any idea how many hours I've spent in psychiatrists' offices? My mom's convinced I'm a complete schizo."

"Yes." Father Dominic nodded thoughtfully.

"Yes, I could see how a miraculous gift like ours might be considered by a layperson as—well, unusual."

"Unusual? Are you *kidding* me?"

"I suppose I have been rather sheltered here in the Mission," Father Dominic admitted. "It never occurred to me that it must be extremely difficult for those of you out in the, er, trenches, so to speak, with no real ecclesiastical support—"

"Those of us?" I raised my eyebrows. "You mean there's more than just you and me?"

He looked surprised. "Well, I just assumed . . . surely there must be. We can't be the last of our kind. No, no, surely there are others."

"Excuse me." The ghost looked at us very sarcastically. "But would you mind telling me what's going on here? Who is this bitch? Is she the one taking my place?"

"Hey! Watch your mouth." I shot her a dirty look. "This guy's a priest, you know."

She sneered at me. "Uh, duh. I *know* he's a priest. He's only been trying to get rid of me all week."

I glanced at Father Dominic in surprise, and he said, looking embarrassed, "Well, you see, Heather's being a bit obstinate—"

"If you think," Heather said, in her snotty little

voice, "that I'm going to just stand back and let you assign my locker to this bitch—"

"Call me a bitch one more time, missy," I said, "and I'll make sure you spend the rest of eternity inside this locker of yours."

Heather looked at me without the slightest trace of fear. "Bitch," she said, stretching the word out so it contained multiple syllables.

I hit her so fast she never saw my fist coming. I hit her hard, hard enough to send her reeling into the line of lockers and leave a long, body-shaped dent in them. She landed hard, too, on the stone floor, but was on her feet again a second later. I expected her to strike back at me, but instead, Heather got up and, with a whimper, ran for all she was worth down the corridor.

"Huh," I said, mostly to myself. *"Chicken."*

She'd be back, of course. I'd only startled her. She'd be back. But hopefully when I saw her again, she'd have a slightly improved attitude.

Heather gone, I blew lightly on my knuckles. Ghosts have surprisingly bony jaws.

"So," I said. "What were you saying, Father?"

Father Dominic, still staring where Heather had been standing, remarked, pretty dryly for a priest, "Interesting mediation techniques they're teaching out east these days."

"Hey," I said. "Nobody calls me names and gets away with it. I don't care how tortured he was in his past life. Or hers."

"I think," Father Dominic said thoughtfully, "there are some things we need to discuss, you and I."

Then he brought a finger to his lips. To one side of us a door opened and a large man, his face heavily bearded, looked out into the breezeway, having heard the crash of Heather's astral body—funny how much the dead can weigh—hitting the row of lockers.

"Everything all right, Dom?" he asked, when he saw Father Dominic.

"Everything's fine, Carl," Father Dominic said. "Just fine. And look what I've brought you." Father Dominic placed a hand on my shoulder. "Your newest pupil, Susannah Simon. Susannah, meet your homeroom teacher, Carl Walden."

I stuck out the hand I'd just knocked Heather senseless with. "How do you do, Mr. Walden?"

"Just fine, Miss Simon. Just fine." Mr. Walden's enormous hand engulfed mine. He didn't look much like a teacher to me. He looked more like a lumberjack. In fact, he practically had to flatten himself against the wall to give me room to slip past him into his classroom. "Nice to have you with us," he said in his big, booming voice. "Thanks, Dom, for bringing her over."

"Not a problem," Father Dominic said. "We were just having a little difficulty with her locker. You probably heard it. Didn't mean to disturb you. I'll have the custodian look into it. In the meantime, Susannah, I'll expect you back in my office at three, to, um, fill out the rest of those forms."

I smiled at him sweetly. "Oh, no can do, Father. My ride leaves at three."

Father Dominic scowled at me. "Then I'll send you a pass. Expect one around two."

"Okay," I said, and waggled my fingers at him. "Buh-bye."

I guess on the West Coast you aren't supposed to say buh-bye to the principal, or waggle your fingers at him, since when I turned around to face my new classmates, they were all staring at me with their mouths hanging open.

Maybe it was my outfit. I had worn a little bit more black than usual, due to nerves. When in doubt, I always say, wear black. You can never go wrong with black.

Or maybe you can. Because as I looked around at the gaping faces, I didn't see a single black garment in the lot. A lot of white, a few browns, and a heck of a lot of khaki, but no black.

Oops.

Mr. Walden didn't seem to notice my discomfort. He introduced me to the class, and made me tell them where I came from. I told them, and they all stared at me blankly. I began to feel sweat pricking the back of my neck. I have to tell you, sometimes I prefer the company of the undead to the company of my peers. Sixteen-year-olds can be really scary.

But Mr. Walden was a good guy. He only made me stand there a minute, under all those stares, and then he told me to take a seat.

This sounds like a simple thing, right? Just go and take a seat. But you see, there were two seats. One was next to this really pretty tanned girl, with thick, curly, honey-blond hair. The other was way in the back, behind a girl with hair so white, and skin so pink, she could only be an albino.

No, I am not kidding. An *albino*.

Two things influenced my decision. One was that when I saw the seat in the back, I also happened to see that the windows, directly behind that seat, looked out across the school parking lot.

Okay, not such an inspiring view, you might say. But beyond the parking lot was the sea.

I am not kidding. This school, my new school, had a view of the Pacific that was even better than the one in my bedroom since the school was so much closer to the beach. You could actually see the waves from my homeroom's windows. I wanted to sit as close to the window as possible.

The second reason I sat there was simple: I didn't want to take the seat by the tan girl and have the albino girl think I'd done it because I didn't want to sit near anyone as weird looking as she was. Stupid, right? Like she'd even care what I did. But I didn't even hesitate. I saw the sea, I saw the albino, and I went for it.

As soon as I sat down, of course, this girl a few seats away snickered and went, under her breath, but perfectly audibly, "God, sit by the freak, why don't you."

I looked at her. She had perfectly curled hair and perfectly made-up eyes. I said, not talking under my breath at all, "Excuse me, do you have Tourette's?"

Mr. Walden had turned around to write something on the board, but the sound of my voice stopped him. Everybody turned around to look at me, including the girl who'd spoken. She blinked at me, startled. "What?"

"Tourette's Syndrome," I said. "It's a neurological disorder that causes people to say things they don't really mean. Do you have it?"

The girl's cheeks had slowly started turning scarlet. "No."

"Oh," I said. "So you were being purposefully rude."

"I wasn't calling *you* a freak," the girl said quickly.

"I'm aware of that," I said. "That's why I'm only going to break *one* of your fingers after school, instead of *all* of them."

She spun around real fast to face the front of the classroom. I settled back into my chair. I don't know what everybody started buzzing about after that, but I did see the albino's scalp—which was plainly visible beneath the white of her hair—turn a deep magenta with embarrassment. Mr. Walden had to call everyone to order, and when people ignored him, he slammed his fist down on his desk and told us that if we had so damned much to say, we could say it in a thousand-word essay on the battle at Bladensburg during the War of 1812, double-spaced, and due on his desk first thing tomorrow morning.

Oh well. Good thing I wasn't in school to make friends.

# chapter *seven*

And yet I did. Make friends, I mean.

I didn't try to. I didn't even really want to. I mean, I have enough friends back in Brooklyn. I have Gina, the best friend anybody could have. I didn't need any more friends than that.

And I really didn't think anybody here was going to like me—not after having been assigned a thousand-word essay because of what happened when I sat down. And especially not after what happened when we were informed that it was time for second period—there was no bell system at the Mission School, we changed class on the hour, and had five minutes to get to where we were going. No sooner had Mr. Walden dismissed us than the albino girl turned around in her seat and asked, her purple eyes glowing furiously behind the tinted lenses of her glasses, "Am I supposed to be grateful to you, or something, for what you said to Debbie?"

"You," I said, standing up, "aren't supposed to be anything, as far as I'm concerned."

She stood up, too. "But that's why you did it, right? Defended the albino? Because you felt sorry for me?"

"I did it," I said, folding my coat over my arm, "because Debbie is a troll."

I saw the corners of her lips twitch. Debbie had swept up her books and practically run for the door the minute Mr. Walden had dismissed us. She and a bunch of other girls, including the pretty tanned one who'd had the empty seat next to her, were whispering among themselves and casting me dirty looks over their Ralph Lauren sweater–draped shoulders.

I could tell the albino girl wanted to laugh at my calling Debbie a troll, but she wouldn't let herself. She said fiercely, "I can fight my own battles, you know. I don't need your help, New York."

I shrugged. "Fine with me, Carmel."

She couldn't help smiling then. When she did,

she revealed a mouthful of braces that winked as brightly as the sea outside the window. "It's CeeCee," she said.

"What's CeeCee?"

"My name. I'm CeeCee." She stuck out a milky-white hand, the nails of which were painted a violent orange. "Welcome to the Mission Academy."

At 9:00, Mr. Walden had dismissed us. By 9:02, CeeCee had introduced me to twenty other people, most of whom trotted after me as we moved to our next class, wanting to know what it was like to have lived in New York City.

"Is it really," one horsey-looking girl asked wistfully, "as . . . as . . ." She struggled to think of the word she was looking for. "As . . . *metropolitan* as they all say?"

These girls, I probably don't have to add, were not the class lookers. They were not, I saw at once, on speaking terms with the pretty tanned girl and the one whose fingers I'd threatened to break after school, who were the ones so well-turned out in their sweater sets and khaki skirts. Oh, no. The girls who came up to me were a motley bunch, some acned, some overweight, or way way too skinny. I was horrified to see that one was wearing open-toe shoes with reinforced toe pantyhose. Beige pantyhose, too. And white shoes. In January!

I could see I was going to have my work cut out for me.

CeeCee appeared to be the leader of their little pack. Editor of the school paper, the *Mission News,* which she called "more of a literary review than an actual newspaper," CeeCee had been in earnest when she'd informed me she did not need me to fight her battles for her. She had plenty of ammunition of her own, including a pretty packed arsenal of verbal zingers and an extremely serious work ethic. Practically the first thing she asked me—after she got over being mad at me—was if I'd be interested in writing a piece for her paper.

"Nothing fancy," she said airily. "Maybe just an essay comparing East Coast and West Coast teen culture. I'm sure you must see a lot of differences between us and your friends back in New York. Whaddaya say? My readers would be plenty interested—especially girls like Kelly and Debbie. Maybe you could slip in something about how on the East Coast being tan is like a *faux pas*."

Then she laughed, not sounding evil exactly, but definitely not innocent, either. But that, I soon realized, was CeeCee, all bright smiles—made brighter by those wicked-looking braces—and bouncy good humor. She was as famous, apparently, for her wisecracking as for her big horse-laugh, which sometimes bubbled out of her when she couldn't control it, and rang out with unabashed joy, and was inevitably hushed by the prissy novices who acted as hall monitors, keeping us from bothering the tourists who came to snap pictures of Junipero Serra being fawned over by those poor bronze Indian women.

The Mission Academy was a small one. There were only seventy sophomores. I was thankful that Dopey and I had conflicting schedules, so that the only period we shared in common was lunch. Lunch, by the way, was conducted in the school yard, which was to one side of the parking lot, a huge grassy playground overlooking the sea, with seniors slumping on the same benches as second graders, and seagulls converging on anyone foolish enough to toss out a fry. I know because I tried it. Sister Ernestine—the one Adam, who was in my social studies class, it turned out, had called a broad—came up to me and told me never to do it again. As if I hadn't gotten the point the minute fifty giant squawking gulls came swooping down from the sky and surrounded me, the way the pigeons used to in Washington Square Park if you were foolish enough to throw out a bit of pretzel.

Anyway, Sleepy and Doc shared my lunch period, too. That was the only time I saw any of the Ackermans at school. It was interesting to observe them in their native environment. I was pleased to see that I had been correct in my estimation of their characters. Doc hung with a crowd of extremely nerdy-looking kids, most of whom wore glasses and actually balanced their laptop computers on their laps, something I'd never thought was actually done. Dopey hung with the jocks, around whom flocked—the way the seagulls had flocked around me—the pretty tanned girls in our class, including the one I'd eschewed sitting beside. Their conversation seemed to consist of what they'd gotten for Christmas, this being their first day back from winter break, and who'd broken the most limbs skiing in Tahoe.

Sleepy was perhaps the most interesting, however. Not that he woke up. Please. But he sat at one of the picnic tables with his eyes closed and his face turned to the sun. Since I can see this at home, this was not what interested me. No, what interested me was what was going on beside Sleepy. And that was an incredibly good-looking boy who did nothing but stare straight ahead of him with a look of abject sadness on his face. Occasionally, girls would walk by—as girls will when there is a good-looking boy nearby—and say hi to him, and he'd tear his eyes away from the sea—which was what he was staring at—and say, "Oh, hi," to them before turning his gaze back to those hypnotic waves.

It occurred to me that Sleepy and his friend might very well be potheads. It would explain a lot about Sleepy.

But when I asked CeeCee if she knew who the guy was, and whether or not he had a drug problem, she said, "Oh, that's Bryce Martinson. No, he's not on drugs. He's just sad, you know, 'cause his girlfriend died over the break."

"Really?" I chewed on my corn dog. The food service at the Mission Academy left a lot to be desired. I could see now why so many kids brought their own. Today's entree had been hot dogs. I am not kidding. Hot dogs. "How'd she die?"

"Put a bullet in her brain." Adam, the kid from the principal's office, had joined us. He was eating Chee-tos from a giant bag he'd pulled from a leather backpack. A Louis Vuitton backpack, I might add. "Blew the back of her head away."

One of the horsey girls turned around, having overheard, and went, "God, Adam. How cold can you get?"

Adam shrugged. "Hey. I didn't like her when she was alive. I'm not gonna say I liked her now just because she's dead. In fact, if anything, I hate her more. I heard we're all going to have to do the Stations of the Cross for her on Wednesday."

"Right." CeeCee looked disgusted. "We have to pray for her immortal soul since she committed suicide and is destined to burn in hell for all eternity now."

Adam looked thoughtful. "Really? I thought suicides went to Purgatory."

"No, stupid. Why do you think Monsignor Constantine won't let Kelly have her dumb memorial service? Suicide is a mortal sin. Monsignor Constantine won't allow a suicide to be memorialized in his church. He won't even let her parents bury her in consecrated ground." CeeCee rolled her violet eyes. "I never liked Heather, but I *hate* Monsignor Constantine and his stupid rules even more. I'm thinking of doing an article about it, and calling it 'Father, Son, and the Holy Hypocrite.'"

The other girls tittered nervously. I waited until they were done and then I asked, "Why'd she kill herself?"

Adam looked bored. "Because of Bryce, of course. He broke up with her."

A pretty black girl named Bernadette, who towered over the rest of us at six feet, leaned down to whisper, "I heard he did it at the mall. Can you believe it?"

Another girl said, "Yeah, on Christmas Eve. They were Christmas shopping with each other, and she pointed to this diamond ring in the window at Bergdorf's, and was, like, 'I want that.' And I guess he freaked—you know, it was clearly an engagement ring—and broke up with her on the spot."

"And so she went home and shot herself?" I found this story extremely far-fetched. When I'd asked CeeCee where we were supposed to have lunch if, God forbid, it should happen to rain, she told me that everyone had to sit in their homeroom and eat, and the nuns brought out board games like Parcheesi for people to play. I was wondering if this story, like the one about rainyday lunches, was an invention. CeeCee was exactly the kind of girl who would get a kick out of lying to the new kid—not out of maliciousness, but just to amuse herself.

"Not then," CeeCee said. "She tried to get back together with him for a while. She called him like every ten minutes, until finally his mother told her not to call anymore. Then she started sending him letters, telling him what she was going to do—you know, kill herself if he didn't get back together with her. When he didn't respond, she got her dad's forty-four and drove to Bryce's house and rang the bell."

Adam took up the narrative at this point, so I knew gore was probably going to be involved. "Yeah," he said, standing up so that he could act it, using a Chee-to as the gun. "The Martinsons were having a New Year's party—it was New Year's Eve—so they were home and everything. They opened up the door, and there was this crazy girl on their porch, with a gun to her head. She said if they didn't get Bryce, she was going to pull the trigger. But they couldn't get Bryce, because they'd sent him to Antigua—"

"—Hoping a little sun and surf would soothe his frazzled nerves," CeeCee put in, "because, you know, he's got his college apps to worry about right now. He doesn't need to have the added pressure of a stalker."

Adam glared at her, and went on, holding the

Chee-to to the side of his head. "Yeah, well, that was a gross error on the part of the Martinsons. As soon as she heard Bryce was out of the country, she pulled the trigger, and blew out the back of her skull, and bits of her brain and stuff stuck to the Christmas lights the Martinsons had strung up."

Everyone but me groaned at this particular detail. I had other things on my mind, however. "The empty chair in homeroom. The one by what's-her-name—Kelly. That was the dead girl's seat, wasn't it?"

Bernadette nodded. "Yeah. That's why we thought it was so weird when you walked past it. It was like you *knew* that that was where Heather had sat. We all thought maybe you were psychic or something—"

I didn't bother telling them that the reason I hadn't sat in Heather's seat had nothing whatsoever to do with being psychic. I didn't say anything, actually. I was thinking, *Gee, Mom, nice of you to tell me why there was suddenly this space for me, when before the school had been too crowded to let in another new student.*

I stared at Bryce. He was tanned from his trip to Antigua. He sat on the picnic table with his feet on the bench, his elbows on his knees, staring out at the Pacific. A gentle wind tugged at some of his sandy-blond hair.

*He has no idea*, I thought. *He has no idea at all. He thinks his life is bad now? Just wait.*

*Just wait.*

# chapter eight

He didn't have to wait long. In fact, it was right after lunch that she came after him. Not that he ever knew it, of course. I spotted her immediately in the crowd as everybody headed toward their lockers. Ghosts have a sort of glow about them that sets them apart from the living—thank God, too, or half the time I might never have known the difference.

Anyway, there she was staring daggers at him like one of those blond kids out of *Village of the Damned*. People, not knowing she was there, kept walking straight through her. I sort of envied them. I wish ghosts were invisible to me like they were to everybody else. I know that would mean

I wouldn't have been able to enjoy my dad's company these past few years, but, hey, it also would have meant I wouldn't be standing there knowing Heather was about to do something horrible.

Not that I knew what it was she planned on doing to him. Ghosts can get pretty rough sometimes. The trick Jesse had done with the mirror was nothing, really. I've had objects thrown at me with enough force that, if I hadn't ducked, I'd certainly be one with the spirit world as well. I've had concussions and broken bones galore. My mom just thinks I'm accident-prone. Yeah, Mom. That's right. I broke my wrist falling down the stairs. Oh, and the reason I fell down the stairs is that the ghost of a three-hundred-year-old conquistador pushed me.

The minute I saw Heather, though, I knew she was up to no good. I was not basing this assumption on my previous interaction with her. Oh, no. See, I followed the direction of Heather's gaze, and saw that it wasn't Bryce, exactly, that she was staring at. It was actually one of the rafters in the section of breezeway beneath which Bryce was walking that had attracted her attention. And, as I stood there, I saw the timber start to shake. Not the whole breezeway. Oh, no. Just one single, heavy piece. The piece directly over Bryce's head.

I acted without thought. I threw myself as hard as I could at Bryce. We both went flying. And good thing, too. Because we were still rolling when I heard an enormous explosion. I ducked my head to shield my eyes, so I didn't actually see the piece of timber explode. But I heard it. And I felt it, too. Those tiny splinters of wood *hurt* as they pelted me. Good thing I was wearing wool slacks, too.

Bryce lay so still beneath me that I thought maybe a chunk of wood had got him between the frontal lobes, or something. But when I lifted my face from his chest, I saw that he was okay—he was just staring, horrified, at the ten-inch-thick plank of wood, nearly two feet long, that lay a few feet away from us. All around us were scattered shards of wood that had broken off the main piece. I guess Bryce was realizing that if that plank had succeeded in splintering his cranium, there'd have been little pieces of Bryce scattered all around that stone floor, too.

"Excuse me. Excuse me—" I heard Father Dominic's strained voice, and saw him push through the crowd of stunned onlookers. He froze when he saw the chunk of wood, but when his gaze took in Bryce and me, he sprung into action again.

"Good God in heaven," he cried, hurrying toward us. "Are you children all right? Susannah, are you hurt? Bryce?"

I sat up slowly. I frequently have to check for broken bones, and have found, over the years, that the slower you get up, the more chance you have at discovering what's broken, and the less chance there is you'll put weight on it.

But in this particular case, nothing seemed broken. I got to my feet.

"Good gracious," Father Dom was saying. "Are you sure you're all right?"

"I'm fine," I said, brushing myself off. There were little pieces of wood all over me. And this was my best Donna Karan jacket. I looked around for Heather—really, if I'd have found her at that particular moment, I'd have killed her, I really would have . . . except, of course, that she's already dead. But she was gone.

"God," Bryce said, coming up to me. He didn't look hurt, just shaken up a little. Actually, it would have been hard to hurt a guy as big as he was. He was six feet tall and broad shouldered, a genuine Baldwin.

And he was talking to me. *Me!*

"God, are you okay?" he wanted to know. "Thank you. God. I think you must have saved my life."

"Oh," I said. "It was nothing, really." I couldn't resist reaching out and plucking a splinter of wood from his sweater vest. Cashmere. Just as I'd suspected.

"What is going on here?" A tall guy in a lot of robes with a red beanie on his head came pushing through the crowd. When he saw the wood on the ground, then looked up to take in the gaping hole where it was supposed to be, he turned on Father Dom and said, "See? See, Dominic? This is what comes of you letting your precious birds nest wherever they want! Mr. Ackerman warned us this might happen, and look! He was right! Somebody might have been killed!"

So this, then, was Monsignor Constantine.

"I'm so sorry, Monsignor," Father Dom said. "I can't think how such a thing could have happened. Thank heavens no one was hurt." He turned to Bryce and me. "You two *are* all right? You know, I think Miss Simon looks a little pale. I'll just take her off to see the nurse, if that's all right with you, Susannah. The rest of you children get on to class now. Everyone is all right. It was just an accident. Run along, now."

Amazingly, people did as he said. Father Dominic had that kind of way about him. You just sort of had to do what he said. Thank God he used his powers for good instead of evil!

I wish the same could have been said of the monsignor. He stood in the suddenly empty corridor, staring down at the piece of wood. Anybody could tell just to look at it that it wasn't the least bit rotten. The wood wasn't new by any means, but it was perfectly dry.

"I'm having those bird nests removed, Dominic," the monsignor said bitterly. "All of them. We simply can't take these kinds of risks. Supposing one of the tourists had been standing here? Or, God forbid, the archbishop. He's coming next month, you know. What if Archbishop Rivera had been standing here and this beam had fallen? What then, Dominic?"

The nuns who'd come out, hearing all the ruckus, cast looks of such reproof at poor Father Dominic that I nearly said something. I opened my mouth to do so, in fact, but Father Dom tightened his grip on my arm and started marching me away. "Of course," he called. "You're quite right. I'll get the custodial staff right on it, Monsignor. We couldn't have the archbishop injured. No, indeed."

"God, what a pus-head!" I said, as soon as we were safely behind the closed door to the principal's office. "Is he kidding, thinking a couple of birds could do that?"

Father Dominic had gone straight across the room to a small cabinet in which there were a number of trophies and plaques—teaching awards, I found out later. Before he'd been reassigned by the diocese to an administrative position, Father Dominic had been a popular and much-loved teacher of biology. He reached behind one of the awards and drew out a packet of cigarettes.

"I'm not sure it isn't a bit sacrilegious, Susannah," he said, looking down at the red-and-white pack, "to refer to a monsignor in the Catholic church as a pus-head."

"Good thing I'm not Catholic, then," I said. "And you can smoke one of those if you want to." I nodded at the cigarettes in his hand. "I won't tell."

He looked down longingly at the pack for a minute more, then heaved this big sigh, and put them back where he'd found them. "No," he said. "Thank you, but I'd better not."

Jeez. Maybe it was a good thing I'd never really gotten the hang of the smoking thing.

I thought I'd better change the subject, so I stooped to examine some of the teaching awards. "1964," I said. "You've been around a while."

"I have." Father Dom sat down behind his desk. "What, in heaven's name, happened out there, Susannah?"

"Oh," I shrugged. "That was just Heather. I guess we know now why she's sticking around. She wants to kill Bryce Martinson."

Father Dominic shook his head. "This is terrible. It really is. I've never seen such . . . such violence from a spirit. Never, not in all my years as a mediator."

"Really?" I looked out the window. The principal's office looked, not out to the sea, but toward the hills where I lived. "Hey," I said. "You can see my house from here!"

"And she was always such a sweet girl, too. We never had a disciplinary problem from Heather Chambers, not in all her years at the Mission Academy. What could be causing her to feel so much hatred for a young man she professed to love?"

I glanced at him over my shoulder. "Are you kidding me?"

"Yes, well, I know they broke up, but such extreme emotions—this killing rage she's in. Surely that's quite unusual—"

I shook my head. "Excuse me, I know you took a vow of celibacy and all, but haven't you ever been in love? Don't you know what it's like? That guy hosed her. She thought they were going to get married. I know, that was stupid, especially since she's only what, sixteen? Still, he just hosed her. If that's not enough to inspire a killing rage in a girl, I don't know what is."

He studied me thoughtfully. "You're speaking from experience."

"Who me? Not quite. I mean, I've had crushes on guys and stuff, but I can't say any of them have ever returned the favor." Much to my chagrin. "Still, I can *imagine* how Heather must have felt when he broke up with her."

"Like killing herself, I suppose," Father Dominic said.

"Exactly. But killing herself didn't turn out to be enough. She won't be satisfied until she takes him down with her."

"This is dreadful," Father Dominic said. "Really, really dreadful. I've talked with her until I was blue in the face, and she won't listen. And now, the first day back, this happens. I'm going to have to advise that the young man stay home until we can get this resolved."

I laughed. "How are you going to do that? Tell him his dead girlfriend's trying to kill him? Oh, yeah, that'll go over well with the monsignor."

"Not at all." Father Dom opened a drawer, and started rifling through it. "With a little ingenuity, I can see that Mr. Martinson is out for a solid week or two."

"Oh, no way!" I felt myself go pale. "You're going to poison him? I thought you were a priest! Isn't there a rule against that sort of thing?"

"Poison? No, no, Susannah. I was thinking of giving him head lice. The nurse checks for them once a semester. I'll just see that young Mr. Martinson comes down with a bad case of them—"

"Oh my God!" I shrieked. "That's disgusting! You can't put lice in that guy's hair!"

Father Dominic looked up from his drawer. "Why ever not? It will serve our purposes exactly. Keep him out of harm's way long enough for you and I to talk some sense into Miss Chambers, and—"

"You can't put lice in that guy's hair," I said again, more vehemently than was, perhaps, necessary. I don't know why I was so against the idea, except that . . . well, he had such nice hair. I'd gotten a pretty close look at it when we'd been sprawled on the ground together. It was curly, soft-looking hair, the kind of hair I could picture myself running my fingers through. The thought of bugs crawling around in it turned my stomach. How did that kid's rhyme go?

*You gazed into my eyes*
*What could I do but linger?*
*I ran my hands all through your hair*
*And a cootie bit my finger.*

"Aw, jeez," I said, sitting down on top of the desk. "Hold the lice, will you? Let me deal with Heather. You say you've been talking to her for how long now? A week?"

"Since the New Year," Father Dominic said. "Yes. That's when she first showed up here. I can see now she's just been waiting for Bryce."

"Right. Well, let me take care of it. Maybe she just needs a little dose of girl talk."

"I don't know." Father Dominic regarded me a little dubiously. "I really feel that you have a bit of a propensity toward . . . well, toward the physical. The role of a mediator is supposed to be a non-violent one, Susannah. You are supposed to be someone who *helps* troubled spirits, not *hurts* them."

"Hello? Were you out there just now? You think I was just supposed to stand there and *talk* that beam into not crushing that guy's skull?"

"Of course not. I'm just saying that if you tried a little compassion—"

"Hey. I have plenty of compassion, Father. My heart bleeds for this girl, it really does. But this is *my* school. Got it? Mine. Not hers, not anymore. She made her decision, and now she's got to stick with it. And I'm not letting her take Bryce—or anyone else—down with her."

"Well." Father Dominic looked skeptical. "Well, if you're sure . . ."

"Oh, I'm sure." I hopped off his desk. "Just leave it to me, all right?"

Father Dominic said, "All right." But he said it kind of faintly, I noticed. I had to get him to write me a hall pass so I could get back to class without getting busted by one of the nuns. I was waiting for one of them—a pinch-faced novice—to finish scrutinizing this pass before she'd let me go on down the corridor when a side door marked NURSE opened, and out stepped Bryce with a hall pass of his own.

"Hey," I couldn't help blurting out. "What happened? Did she—I mean, did something else happen? Are you hurt?"

He grinned a bit sheepishly. "No. Well, unless you count this wicked splinter I got under my thumbnail. I was trying to brush all those little pieces of wood off my pants, you know, and one of them got under there, and—" He held up his right hand. A large bandage had been wrapped around his thumb.

"Yikes," I said.

"I know." He looked mournful. "She used Mercurochrome, too. I *hate* that stuff."

"Man," I said. "You have had a rotten day."

"Not really," he said, putting his thumb down. "At least, not as bad as it would have been if you hadn't been here. If it weren't for you, I'd be dead." He noticed that I'd come through the door marked PRINCIPAL and asked, "Did you get in trouble or something?"

"No," I said. "Father Dominic just wanted me to fill out some forms. I'm new, you know."

"And as a new student," the novice said severely, "you ought to be made aware that loitering in the halls is not allowed. Both of you had better get to your classes."

I apologized and took back my pass. Bryce very chivalrously offered to show me where my next class was, and the novice went away, seemingly satisfied. As soon as she was out of earshot, Bryce said, "You're Suze, right? Jake told me about you. You're his new stepsister from New York."

"That's me," I said. "And you're Bryce Martinson."

"Oh, Jake's mentioned me?"

I almost laughed out loud at the idea of Sleepy mentioning much of anything. I said, "No, it wasn't Jake."

He said, "Oh," in such a sad voice that I almost felt sorry for him. "I guess people must be talking about me, huh?"

"A little." I took the plunge. "I'm sorry about what happened with your girlfriend."

"So am I, believe me." If he was mad that I'd brought the subject up, you couldn't tell. "I didn't even want to come back here after . . . you know. I tried to transfer to RLS, but they're full. Even the public school didn't want me. It's tough to transfer with only one semester to go. I wouldn't have come back at all except that . . . well, you know. Colleges generally want you to have graduated from high school before they'll let you in."

I laughed. "I've heard that."

"Anyway." Bryce noticed I was holding my coat—I'd been dragging it around all day since I couldn't use my locker, the door having been dented permanently shut when I'd knocked Heather into it—and said, "Want me to carry that for you?"

I was so shocked by this civility that without even thinking, I said, "Sure," and passed it over to him. He folded it over one arm, and said, "So, I guess everybody must be blaming me for what happened. To Heather, I mean."

"I don't think so," I said. "If anything, people are blaming Heather for what happened to Heather."

"Yeah," Bryce said, "but I mean, I drove her to it, you know? That's the thing. If I just hadn't broken up with her—"

"You have a pretty high opinion of yourself, don't you?"

He looked taken aback. "What?"

"Well, your assumption that she killed herself because you broke up with her. I don't think that's why she killed herself at all. She killed herself because she was sick. You had nothing to do with making her that way. Your breaking up with her may have acted as a sort of catalyst for her final breakdown, but it could just have easily been some other crisis in her life—her parents getting divorced, her not making the cheerleader squad, her cat dying. Anything. So try not to be so hard on yourself." We were at the door to my classroom—geometry, I think it was, with Sister Mary Catherine. I turned to him and took my coat back. "Well, this is my stop. Thanks for the lift."

He held onto one sleeve of my coat. "Hey," he said, looking down at me. It was hard to see his eyes—it was pretty dark beneath the breezeway, shadowed as it was from the sun. But I remembered from when we'd fallen down together that his eyes were blue. A really nice blue. "Hey, listen," he said. "Let me take you out tonight. To thank you for saving my life and everything."

"Thanks," I said, giving my coat a tug. "But I already have plans." I didn't add that my plans involved him in a most intimate manner.

"Tomorrow night, then," he said, still not relinquishing my coat.

"Look," I said, "I'm not allowed to go out on school nights."

This was patently untrue. Except for the fact that the police have brought me home a few times, my mother trusted me implicitly. If I wanted to go out with a boy on a school night, she'd have let me. The thing is, the subject had never really come up, no boy ever having offered to take me out on a school night, or any other for that matter.

Not that I'm a dog or anything. I mean, I'm no Cindy Crawford, but I'm not exactly busted, either. I guess the truth of the matter is, I was always considered something of a weirdo in my old school. Girls who spend a lot of time talking to themselves and getting in trouble with the police generally are.

Don't get me wrong. Occasionally new guys would show up at school, and they'd express some interest in me . . . but only until someone who knew me filled them in. Then they'd avoid me like I had the plague or something.

East Coast boys. What did *they* know?

But now I had a chance to start all over, with a new population of boys who had no idea about my past—well, except for Sleepy and Dopey, and I doubted they would tell since neither of them are what you'd call . . . well, verbal.

Neither of them had evidently gotten to Bryce, anyway, since the next words out of his mouth were, "This weekend, then. What are you doing Saturday night?"

I wasn't sure it was such a good idea to get involved with a guy whose dead girlfriend was trying to kill him. I mean, what if she found out and resented me for it? I was sure Father Dominic wouldn't think it was very cool, me going out with Bryce.

Then again, how often did a girl like me get asked out by a totally hot guy like Bryce Martinson?

"Okay," I said. "Saturday it is. Pick me up at seven?"

He grinned. He had very nice teeth, white and even. "Seven," he said, letting go of my coat. "See you then. If not before."

"See you then." I stood with my hand on the door to Sister Mary Catherine's geometry class. "Oh, and Bryce."

He had started down the breezeway, toward his own classroom. "Yeah?"

"Watch your back."

I think he winked at me, but it was kind of hard to tell in the shade.

# chapter nine

When I climbed into the Rambler at the end of the day, Doc was all over me. "Everybody's talking about it!" he cried, bouncing up and down on the seat. "Everybody saw it! You saved that guy's life! You saved Bryce Martinson's life!"

"I didn't save his life," I said, calmly twisting the rearview mirror so I could see how my hair looked. Perfect. Salt air definitely agrees with me.

"You did so. I saw that big chunk of wood. If that'd landed on his head, it've killed him! You saved him, Suze. You really did."

"Well." I rubbed a little gloss into my lips. "Maybe."

"God, you've only been at the Mission one day,

and already you're the most popular girl in school!"

Doc was completely unable to contain himself. Sometimes I wondered whether Ritalin might have been the answer. Not that I didn't like the kid. In fact, I liked him best out of all of Andy's boys—which I realize is not saying much, but it's all I've got. It had been Doc who, just the night before, had come to me while I'd been trying to decide what to wear my first day at school and asked me, his face very pale, if I was sure I didn't want to trade bedrooms with him.

I'd looked at him like he was nuts. Doc had a nice room, and everything, but please. Give up my private bath and sea view? No way. Not even if it meant ridding myself of my unwanted roommate, Jesse, whom I hadn't actually heard from since I'd told him to get the hell out.

"What on earth makes you think I'd want to give up my room?" I asked him.

Doc shrugged. "Just that . . . well, this room's kinda creepy, don't you think?"

I stared at him. You should have seen my room just then. With the bedside lamp on, casting a cheerful pink glow over everything, and my CD player belting out Janet Jackson—loud enough that my mother had shouted twice for me to turn it down—creepy was the last thing anyone would have called my room. "Creepy?" I echoed, looking around. No sign of Jesse. No sign of anything at all undead. We were quite firmly in the realm of the living. "What's creepy about it?"

Doc pursed his lips. "Don't tell my dad," he said, "but I've been doing a lot of research into this house, and I've come to the conclusion—quite a definitive one—that it's haunted."

I blinked at his freckled little face, and saw that he was serious. *Quite* serious, as his next remark proved.

"Although modern scientists have, for the most part, debunked the majority of claims of paranormal activity in this country, there is still ample evidence that unexplained spectral phenomena exist in our world. My own personal investigation of this house was unsatisfactory insofar as traditional indications of a spiritual presence, such as the so-called cold spot. But there was nevertheless a very definite fluctuation of temperature in this room, Suze, leading me to believe that it was probably the scene of at least one incidence of great violence—perhaps even a murder—and that some remnant of the victim—call it the soul, if you will—still lurks here, perhaps in the vain hope of gaining justice for his untimely death."

I leaned against one of the posts of my bedframe. I had to, or I might have fallen down. "Gee," I said, keeping my voice steady with an effort. "Way to make a girl feel welcome."

Doc looked embarrassed. "I'm sorry," he said, the tips of his sticky-outy ears turning red. "I shouldn't have said anything. I did mention it to Jake and Brad, and they told me I was nuts. I probably am." He swallowed bravely. "But I feel it's my duty, as a man, to offer to trade rooms with you. You see, I'm not afraid."

I smiled at him, my shock forgotten in a sudden rush of affection for him. I was really touched. You could see the offer had taken all the guts the little guy had. He really and truly believed my room was haunted, in spite of everything that science told him, and yet he'd been willing to sacrifice himself for my sake, out of some sort of inborn chivalry. You had to like the little guy. You really did.

"That's okay, Doc," I said, forgetting myself in a sudden burst of sentimentality and calling him by my own private nickname for him. "I think I can pretty much handle any paranormal phenomena that might occur around here."

He didn't seem to mind the new nickname,

though. He said, obviously relieved, "Well, if you really don't mind—"

"No, it's okay. But let me ask you something." I lowered my voice, just in case Jesse was lurking around somewhere. "In all of your extensive research, did you ever come across the name of this poor slob whose soul is inhabiting my room?"

Doc shook his head. "Actually, I'm sure I could get it for you, if you really want it. I can look it up down at the library. They have all the newspapers ever printed in the area since the first press started running, shortly before this house was built. It's on microfiche, but I'm sure if I spend enough time looking—"

It seemed kind of wacky to me, some kid spending all his time in a dark library basement looking at microfiche, when a block or two away was this beautiful beach. But hey, to each his own, right?

"Cool," was all I said, however.

Now I could see that Doc's little crush on me was threatening to get blown all out of proportion. First I'd willingly volunteered to abide in a room rumored to be haunted, and then I'd gone and saved Bryce Martinson's life. What was I going to do next? Run a three-minute mile?

"Look," I said, as Sleepy struggled with the ignition, which apparently had a tendency not to work on the first try. "I just did what any of you would have done if you'd been standing nearby."

"Brad *was* standing nearby," Doc said, "and he didn't do anything."

Dopey said, "Jesus Christ, I didn't *see* the stupid beam, okay? If I'd seen it, I'd have pushed him out of the way, too. Christ!"

"Yeah, but you didn't see it. You were probably too busy looking at Kelly Prescott."

This earned Doc a hard slug on the arm. "Shuddup, David," Dopey said. "You don't know anything about it."

"*All* of you shut up," Sleepy said with uncharacteristic grumpiness. "I'll never get this damned car started if you all don't keep distracting me. Brad, stop hitting David, David stop yelling in my ear, and Suze, if you don't move your big head out of the mirror I'll never be able to see where the hell we're going. Damn, I can't *wait* till I get that Camaro!"

The phone call came after dinner. My mother had to scream up the stairs at me because I had my headphones on. Even though it was only the first day of the new semester, I had a lot of homework to do, especially in geometry. We'd only been on Chapter Seven back in my old school. The Mission Academy sophomores were already on Chapter Twelve. I knew I was pretty much dead meat if I didn't start trying to catch up.

When I came downstairs to pick up the phone, my mom was already so mad at me for making her scream—she has to watch her vocal chords for her job and everything—that she wouldn't tell me who it was. I picked up the receiver and went, "Hello?"

There was a pause, and then Father Dominic's voice came on. "Hello? Susannah? Is that you? Look, I'm sorry to bother you at home, but I've been giving this some thought and I really think—yes, I really do think we need to do something right away. I can't stop thinking about what might have happened to poor Bryce if you hadn't been there."

I looked over my shoulder. Dopey was playing Cool Boarders—with his dad, the only person in the house who let him win—my mom was working on her computer, Sleepy was out subbing for some pizza deliverer who'd called in sick, and Doc was sitting at the dining room table working on a science project that wasn't due until April.

"Uh," I said. "Look. I can't really talk right now."

"I realize that," Father Dom said. "And don't worry—I had one of the novices ask for you. Your mother thinks it's just some new little friend you've made at school. But the thing of it is, Susannah, we've got to do something, and I think it had better be tonight—"

"Look," I said. "Don't worry about it. I've got it under control."

Father Dom sounded surprised. "You do? You *do*? *How? How* have you got it under control?"

"Never mind. But I've done this before. Everything will be fine. I promise."

"Yes, well, it's all very well to promise everything will be fine, but I've seen you at work, Susannah, and I can't say I've been very impressed with your technique. We've got the archbishop visiting in a month, and I can't very well—"

The call-waiting went off. I said, "Oh, hang on a sec. I've got another call." I hit the hook and went, "Ackerman-Simon residence."

"Suze?" A boy's voice, unrecognizable to me.

"Yes. . . ."

"Oh, hi. It's Bryce. So. What's going on?"

I looked at my mother. She was scowling into the story she was working on. "Um," I said. "Nothing much. Can you hold on a second, Bryce? I've got someone on the other line."

"Sure," Bryce said.

I switched back to Father Dominic. "Uh, hi," I said, careful not to say his name. "I gotta go. My mother has a very important caller on the other line. A senator.. State senator." I was probably going to go to hell for it—if there was such a place—but I couldn't very well tell Father Dominic the truth: that I was dating the ghost's ex-boyfriend.

"Oh, of course," Father Dominic said. "I—well, if you have a plan."

"I do. Don't worry. Nothing will ruin the archbishop's visit. I promise. Bye." I hung up and got back to Bryce. "Uh, hi. Sorry about that. What's up?"

"Oh, nothing. I was just thinking about you. What do you want to do on Saturday? I mean, do you want to go to dinner, or to a movie, or both, maybe?"

The other line went off. I said, "Bryce, I'm really sorry, it's a zoo here, could you hang on a minute? Thanks. Hello?"

A girl's voice I'd never heard before said, "Oh, hi, is this Suze?"

"Speaking," I said.

"Oh, hi, Susie. It's Kelly. Kelly Prescott, from your homeroom? Listen, I just wanted to let you know—what you did today for Bryce—that was so righteous. I mean, I have never in my life seen anything so brave. They should totally put you on the news or something. Anyway, I'm having a little get-together at my place this Saturday—nothing much, just a pool party, my folks'll be out of town, and our pool's heated, of course—so I thought, if you wanted, maybe you could stop by."

I stood there, holding the phone, totally stunned. Kelly Prescott, the richest, most beautiful girl in the entire sophomore class was inviting me to a pool party on the same night I was going out on a date with the sexiest boy in school. Who happened to be on the other line.

"Yeah, sure, Kelly," I said. "I'd love to. Does Brad know where it is?"

"Brad?" Kelly said. Then, "Oh, *Brad.* That's right, he's your half brother or something, right? Oh, yeah, bring him. Listen—"

"I'd love to chat, Kelly, but I got somebody on the other line. Can I talk to you about it tomorrow in school?"

"Oh, totally. Bye."

I clicked back to Bryce, asked him to hold on another second, put my hand over the mouthpiece and yelled, "Brad, pool party at Kelly

Prescott's this Saturday. Be there or be square."

Dopey dropped his joystick. "No way!" he yelled joyfully. "No freakin' way!"

"Hey!" Andy rapped him on the head. "Watch the language."

I got back on with Bryce. "Dinner would be great," I said. "Anything but health food."

Bryce went, "Great! Yeah, I hate health food, too. There's nothing like a really good piece of meat, you know, with some fries on the side, and some gravy—"

"Uh, yeah, right, Bryce. Listen, that's my call-waiting again, I'm really sorry, but I have to go, okay? I'll talk to you tomorrow in school."

"Oh. Okay." Bryce sounded taken aback. I guess I was the first girl who'd ever answered her call-waiting when he was on the line. "Bye, Suze. And, uh, thanks again."

"No problem. Anytime." I hit the receiver. "Hello?"

"Suze! It's CeeCee!"

In the background, I heard Adam yell, "And me, too!"

"Hey, girlfriend," CeeCee said, "we're heading down to the Clutch. Want us to pick you up? Adam just got his license."

"I'm legal!" Adam shouted into the phone.

"The Clutch?"

"Yeah, the Coffee Clutch, downtown. You drink coffee, don't you? I mean, aren't you, like, from New York?"

I had to think about that one. "Uh, yeah. The thing is—I sort of have something I have to do."

"Oh, come *on*. What do you have to do? Wash your cape? I mean, I know you're a big hero and all of that, and probably don't have time for us little people, but—"

"I haven't finished my thousand-word essay on the battle of Bladensburg for Mr. Walden," I said. "And I've got a lot of geometry to do if I'm going to catch up to you geniuses."

"Oh, gawd," CeeCee said. "All *right*. But you have to promise to sit by us at lunch tomorrow. We want to hear all about how you pressed your body up against Bryce's and what it felt like and all that stuff."

"*I* don't," Adam declared, sounding horrified.

"Okay," CeeCee said. "So *I* want to hear all about it."

I assured her I'd spare no detail and hung up. Then I looked down at the phone. To my relief, it did not ring again. I couldn't quite believe it. Never in my life had I been so popular. It was *weird*.

I had lied about my homework, of course. The essay was done, and I had worked through two chapters of geometry—about all I could handle in one night. The truth, of course, was that I had an errand to run, and I had a bit of preparation to do for it.

You don't need a whole lot of tools to do a mediation. I mean, all that stuff about crosses and holy water, I guess you need those things to kill a vampire—and I can tell you right now that I have never in my life met a vampire, and I've spent *a lot* of time in graveyards—but for ghosts, well, you sort of have to wing it.

Sometimes, though, to get the job done right, you have to do a little breaking and entering. For that you need some tools. I highly recommend just using stuff you find on site because then you don't have a lot to carry. But I do have a tool belt with a flashlight and some screwdrivers and pliers and stuff, which I wear over a pair of black leggings. I was fastening this on at around midnight, satisfied that everyone else in the house was asleep—including Sleepy, who was back from his pizza round by then—and had just shrugged into my motorcycle jacket when I got a visit from good old you-know-who.

"Jeez," I said, when I caught a glimpse of his

reflection behind mine in the mirror into which I was primping. I swear, I've been seeing ghosts for years, but it still freaks me out every time one of them materializes in front of me. I spun around, angry not so much that he was there, but because he'd managed to catch me so unaware. "Why are you still hanging around? I thought I told you to get lost."

Jesse was leaning very casually against one of the posts to my bed. His dark-eyed gaze roved from the top of my hooded head to the toes of my black high-tops. "It's a little late to be going out, don't you think, Susannah?" he asked as conversationally as if we'd been in the middle of a discussion about, oh, I don't know, the second Fugitive Slave Act, which I believe had been enacted at or around the time he'd died.

"Uh," I said, pulling the hood back. "Look, no offense, Jesse, but this is my room. How about you try getting out of it? And my business, too, please?"

Jesse didn't move. "Your mother won't like your going out so late at night."

"My mother." I glared at him. Up at him, I should say. He was really disconcertingly tall for someone who was dead. "What would *you* know about my mother?"

"I like your mother very much," Jesse said calmly. "She is a good woman. You are very lucky to have a mother who loves you so very much. It would upset her, I think, to see you putting yourself in the path of danger."

The path of danger. Right! "Yeah, well, news flash, Jesse. I've been sneaking out at night for a long time, and my mom's never said boo about it before. She knows I can take care of myself."

Okay, a lie, but hey, how was he to know?

"Can you?" Jesse lifted a black eyebrow dubiously. I couldn't help noticing that there was a raised scar sliced through the middle of that eyebrow, like someone had taken a swipe at Jesse's face once with a knife. I sort of understood the feeling. Especially when he let out a chuckle, and said, "I don't think so, *querida.* Not in this case."

I held up both my hands. "Okay. Number one, don't call me stuff in Spanish. Number two, you don't even know where I'm going, so I suggest you just get off my back."

"But I do know where you're going, Susannah. You are going down to the school to talk to the girl who is trying to kill that boy, that boy you seem . . . fond of. But I'm telling you, *querida,* she is too much for you to handle alone. If you must go, you ought to have the priest with you."

I stared at him. I had a feeling my eyes were probably bugging out, but I really couldn't believe it. "What?" I sputtered. "How could you know all that? Are you . . . are you *stalking* me?"

He must have realized from my expression that he'd said the wrong thing, since he straightened up and said, "I don't know what that word means, *stalking*. All I know is that you are walking into harm's way."

"You've been following me," I said, stabbing a finger at him accusingly. "Haven't you? God, Jesse, I already have an older brother, thank you very much. I don't need you going around spying—"

"Oh, yes," Jesse said, very sarcastically. "This brother cares for you very much. Almost as much as he cares about his sleep."

"Hey!" I said, coming, against all odds, to Sleepy's defense. "He works nights, okay? He's saving up for a Camaro!"

Jesse made what I'm quite sure was a rude gesture—back in 1850. "You," he said, "aren't going anywhere."

"Oh, yeah?" I turned heel and stormed toward the door. "Try and stop me, cadaver breath."

He did a good job. My hand was on the doorknob when the deadbolt slid into place. I hadn't even realized before that there was a deadbolt on my door—it must have been an ancient one. The handle to it was gone, and God only knew, the key must have long since been lost.

I stood there for half a minute, staring down at my hand in wonder as it pulled futilely on the knob. Then I took a deep cleansing breath, the way my mom's therapist had suggested. She hadn't meant I should do this when dealing with a stalker ghost. She just meant to do it in general, whenever I was feeling stressed.

But it helped. It helped a lot.

"Okay," I said, turning around. "Jesse. This is way uncool."

Jesse looked pretty uncomfortable. I could tell as soon as I looked at him that he wasn't very happy with what he'd done. Whatever had gotten him killed in his previous life, it wasn't because he was innately cruel, or enjoyed hurting people. He was a good guy. Or at least, he was trying to be.

"I can't," he said. "Susannah. Don't go. This woman—this girl, Heather. She isn't like other spirits you might have known in the past. She's filled with hate. She'll kill you if she can."

I smiled at him encouragingly. "Then it's up to me to get rid of her, right? Come on. Unlock the door now."

He hesitated. For a second, I thought he was going to do it. But he didn't, in the end. He just stood there, looking uncomfortable . . . but firm.

"Suit yourself," I said, and walked around him, straight across the room to the bay window. I put a foot onto the seat Andy had made, and easily lifted the screen in the middle window. I had one leg over the sill when I felt his hand go around my wrist.

I turned to look at him. I couldn't see his face since the light from my bedside lamp was behind him, but I could hear his voice well enough and the soft pleading in it.

"Susannah," he said.

And that was all. Just my name.

I didn't say anything. I couldn't, sort of. I mean, I could—it wasn't like there was a lump in my throat, or anything. I just . . . I don't know.

Instead, I looked down at his hand, which was really big and kind of brown, even against the black leather of my jacket. He had a heck of a grip for a dead guy. Even for a live guy. He saw my gaze drop, and looked where I was looking, and saw his hand holding tight around my wrist.

He let go of me as if my skin had suddenly started to blister or something. I finished climbing out the window. When I had successfully maneuvered my way across the porch roof and down to the ground, I turned to look up at my bedroom window.

But he was gone of course.

# chapter ten

It was a cool, clear night. The moon was full. Standing in my front yard, I could see it hanging over the sea like a lightbulb—not a hundred watter, like the sun, but maybe one of those twenty-five dealies you put in those swivel-neck desk lamps. The Pacific, looking smooth as glass from this distance, was black, except for a narrow band of reflected light from the moon, which was white as paper.

I could see in the moonlight the red dome of the Mission's church. But just because I could see the Mission, didn't mean the Mission was nearby. It was a good two miles away. In my pocket were the keys to the Rambler, which I'd snitched a half hour earlier. The metal was warm from the heat of my body. The Rambler, which was turquoise in daylight, looked gray as it sat in the shadow of the driveway.

Hey, I *know* I don't have a license. But if Dopey can do it . . .

Okay. So I chickened out. Look, isn't it better I chose not to drive? I mean, not knowing how and all. Not that I don't know how. Of course I know how to drive. I just haven't had a whole lot of practice, having lived all my life in the public transportation capital of the world. . . .

Oh, never mind. I turned around and started heading for the garage. There had to be a bike around somewhere. Three boys, right? There had to be at least one bike.

I found one. It was a boy's bike, of course, with that stupid bar, and a *really* hard, really skinny seat. But it seemed to work all right. At least the tires weren't flat.

Then I thought, *Okay, girl dressed in black, riding a bike on the streets after midnight, what do I need?*

I didn't think I was going to find any reflective tape, but I thought maybe a bike helmet might do the trick. There was one hanging on a peg on the side of the garage. I put down the hood of my sweatshirt, and fastened the thing on. Oh, yeah. Stylish and safety conscious, that's me.

And then I was off, rolling down the driveway—okay, gravel is not the easiest stuff to ride a bike on, especially going downhill. And the whole way turned out to be downhill since the house looking out over the bay, was perched on the side of this mountainy kind of thing. Going downhill was certainly better than going uphill—there was no way I was ever going to be able to ride back up this thing; I had a pretty good idea I'd be doing some pushing on my way home—but going downhill was pretty harrowing. I mean, the hill was so steep, the way so twisty, and the night air so cold, that I rode with my heart in my throat practically the whole time, tears streaming down the sides of my cheeks because of the wind. And those potholes—

God! Did that stupid seat hurt when I hit a pothole.

But the hill wasn't the worst of it. When I got down the hill I hit an intersection. This was much scarier than the hill because even though it was after midnight, there were cars there. One of them honked at me. But it wasn't my fault. I was going so fast, because of the hill and all, that if I'd stopped I'd probably have gone right over the handlebars. So I kept on going, narrowly avoiding getting hit by a pickup, and then, I don't know how, I was pulling into the school parking lot.

The Mission looked a lot different at night than it did during the day. For one thing, during the day the parking lot was always full, packed with cars belonging to teachers, students, and tourists visiting the church. The lot was empty now, not a single car, and so quiet that you could hear, way off in the distance, the sound of waves hitting Carmel Beach.

The other thing was that, for tourist reasons, I guess, they had set up these spotlights to shine on certain parts of the building, like the dome—it was all lit up—and the front of the church, with its huge arched entranceway. The back of the building, where I pulled up, was pretty dark. Which suited me fine, actually. I hid the bike behind a Dumpster, leaving the helmet dangling from one of the handles, and went up to a window. The Mission was built like a bazillion years ago, back when they didn't have air-conditioning or central heating, so to keep cool in summer and warm in winter, people built their houses really thick. That meant that all the windows in the Mission were set back about a foot into the adobe, with another foot sticking out into the room behind them.

I climbed up onto one of these built-in window seats, looking around first to make sure no one saw me. But there wasn't anybody around except a couple of raccoons that were rooting around the Dumpster for some of the lunch leftovers. Then I cupped my hands over my face, to cut out the light of the moon, and peered inside.

It was Mr. Walden's classroom. With the moonlight flooding into it, I could see his handwriting on the chalkboard, and the big poster of Bob Dylan, his favorite poet, on the wall.

It only took me a second to punch out the glass in one of the old-fashioned iron panes, reach in, and unlatch the window. The hard part about breaking a window isn't the breaking part, or even the reaching in part. It's getting your hand out again that always causes cuts. I had on my best ghost-busting gloves, thick black ones with rubbery stuff on the knuckles, but I've had my sleeve get caught before, and gotten my arm all scratched up.

That didn't happen this time. Plus, the window opened out, instead of up, swinging forward just enough to let a girl like me inside. Occasionally, I've broken in to places that turned out to have alarms—resulting in an uncomfortable ride for me in the back of a car belonging to one of New York's finest—but the Mission hadn't gotten that high-tech with their security system yet. In fact, their security system seemed to consist of locking the doors and windows, and hoping for the best.

Which certainly suited me fine.

Once I was inside Mr. Walden's room, I closed the window behind me. No sense alerting anybody who might happen to be manning the perimeter—as if. It was easy to maneuver between the desks, since the moon was so bright. And once I got the door open and stepped out into the breezeway, I found I didn't need my flashlight, either. The courtyard was flooded with light. I guess the Mission must stay open pretty late for the tourists because there were these big yellow floodlights hidden in the breezeway's eaves, and pointed at various objects of interest: the tallest of the palm trees, the one with the biggest hibiscus bush at its base; the fountain, which was on even though the place was closed; and of course the statue of Father Serra, with one light shining on his bronze head and another on the heads of the Native American women at his feet.

Geesh. It was a good thing Father Serra was good and dead. I had a feeling that statue would have completely embarrassed him.

The breezeway was empty, as was the courtyard. No one was around. All I could hear was the gentle splash of the water in the fountain and the chirping of crickets hidden in the garden. It was a sort of restful place, actually, which was surprising. I mean, none of my other schools had ever struck me as restful. At least, this one did, until this hard voice behind me went, "What are *you* doing here?"

I spun around, and there she was. Just leaning up against her locker—excuse me, *my* locker—and glaring at me, her arms folded across her chest. She was wearing a pair of charcoal-colored slacks—nice ones—and a gray cashmere sweater set. She had an add-a-pearl necklace around her neck, one pearl for every Christmas and birthday she'd been alive, given to her, no doubt, by a set of doting grandparents. On her feet were a pair of shiny black loafers. Her hair, as shiny as her shoes in the yellow light from the floodlamps, looked smooth and golden. She really was a beautiful girl.

Too bad she had blown her head off.

"Heather," I said, pushing the hood of my sweatshirt down. "Hi. I'm sorry to bother you"—it always helps at least to start out polite—"but I really think we need to talk, you and I."

Heather didn't move. Well, that's not true. Her eyes narrowed. They were pale eyes, gray, I think, though it was hard to tell, in spite of the flood-lamps. The long eyelashes—dark with mascara—were tastefully ringed in charcoal liner.

"Talk?" Heather echoed. "Oh, yeah. Like I really want to talk to *you*. I know about you, *Susie*."

I winced. I couldn't help it. "It's Suze," I said.

"Whatever. I know what you're doing here."

"Well, good," I said. "Then I don't have to explain. You want to go sit down, so we can talk?"

"Talk? Why would I want to talk to *you*? What do you think I am, stupid? God, you think you're so sly. You think you can just move right in, don't you?"

I blinked at her. "I beg your pardon?"

"Into my place." She straightened and stepped away from the locker, and walked toward the courtyard as if she were admiring the fountain. "You," she said, tossing me a look over her shoulder. "The new girl. The new girl who thinks she can just slip right into the place I left behind. You've already got my locker. You're on your way to stealing my best friend. I know Kelly called you and asked you to her stupid party. And now you think you can steal my boyfriend."

I put my hands on my hips. "He's not your boyfriend, Heather, remember? He broke up with you. That's why you're dead. You blew your brains out in front of his mother."

Heather's eyes widened. "Shut up," she said.

"You blew your brains out in front of his mother because you were too stupid to realize that no boy—not even Bryce Martinson—is worth dying for." I strolled past her, out onto one of the gravel pathways between the garden beds. I didn't want to admit it, not even to myself, but it was making me a little nervous, standing under the breezeway after what had happened to Bryce. "Boy, you must have been mad when you realized what you'd done. Killed yourself. And over something so stupid. Because of a guy."

"Shut up!" This time she didn't just say it. She screamed it, so loud that she had to ball her hands up into fists at her sides, close her eyes, and hunch up her shoulders to do it. The scream was so loud, my ears were ringing afterward. But no one came running from the rectory, where I saw a few lights on. The mourning doves that I'd heard cooing in the eaves of the breezeway hadn't uttered a peep since Heather had shown up, and the crickets had cut short their midnight serenade.

People can't hear ghosts—well, most people,

anyway—but the same can't be said for animals and even insects. They are hyperalert to the presence of the paranormal. Max, the Ackermans' dog, won't go near my room thanks to Jesse.

"It's no use your screaming like that," I said. "No one but me can hear it."

"I'll scream all I want," she shrieked. And then she proceeded to do so.

Yawning, I went and sat down on one of the wooden benches by Father Serra's statue. There was a plaque, I noticed, at the statue's base. I could read it easily with the help of the floodlamps and the moon.

THE VENERABLE FATHER JUNIPERO SERRA, the plaque read, 1713–1784. HIS RIGHTEOUS WAYS AND SELF-ABNEGATION WERE A LESSON TO ALL WHO KNEW HIM AND RECEIVED HIS TEACHINGS.

Huh. I was going to have to look up self-abnegation in the dictionary when I got home. I wondered if it was the same as self-flagellation, something for which Serra had also been known.

"Are you listening to me?" Heather screamed.

I looked at her. "Do you know what the word *abnegation* means?" I asked.

She stopped screaming and just stared at me. Then she strode forward, her face a mask of livid rage.

"Listen to me, you bitch," she said, stopping when she stood a foot away from me. "I want you gone, do you understand? I want you out of this school. That is *my* locker. Kelly Prescott is *my* best friend. And Bryce Martinson is *my* boyfriend! You get out, you go back to where you came from. Everything was just fine before you got here—"

I had to interrupt. "I'm sorry, Heather, but everything was *not* just fine before I got here. You know how I know that? Because you're dead. Okay? *You are dead.* Dead people don't have lockers, or best friends, or boyfriends. You know why? Because they're dead."

Heather looked as if she was about to start screaming again, but I headed her off at the pass. I said, smoothly and evenly, "Now, I know you made a mistake. You made a horrible, terrible mistake—"

"I'm not the one who made the mistake," Heather said flatly. "Bryce made the mistake. Bryce is the one who broke up with me."

I said, "Yeah, well, that wasn't the mistake I was talking about. I was talking about you shooting yourself because a stupid boy broke up with—"

"If you think he's so stupid," Heather said with

a sneer, "why are you going out with him on Saturday? That's right. I heard him ask you out. The rat. He probably wasn't faithful a day the whole time we were going out."

"Oh," I said. "Well, that's just great. All the more reason for you to kill yourself over him."

There were tears, sparkling like those rhinestones you buy and glue to your fingernails, gathered beneath her lashes. "I loved him," she breathed. "If I couldn't have him, I didn't want to live."

"And now that you're dead," I said tiredly, "you figure he ought to join you, right?"

"I don't like it here," she said softly. "No one can see me. Just you and F-Father Dominic. I get so lonely. . . ."

"Right. That's understandable. But Heather, even if you do manage to kill him, he probably isn't going to like you for it much."

"I can make him like me," Heather said confidently. "After all, it'll just be me and him. He'll have to like me."

I shook my head. "No, Heather. It doesn't work that way."

She stared at me. "What do you mean?"

"If you kill Bryce, there's no guarantee he'll end up here with you. What happens to people after they die—well, I'm not sure, but I think it's different for everyone. If you kill Bryce, he'll go to wherever it is he's supposed to go. Heaven, hell, his next life—I don't know for sure. But I do know he won't end up here with you. It doesn't work that way."

"But—" Heather looked furious. "But that isn't fair!"

"Lots of things aren't fair, Heather. It isn't fair, for example, that you have to suffer for all eternity for a mistake that you made in the heat of a moment. I'm sure if you'd known what it was like to be dead, you never would have killed yourself. But, Heather, it doesn't have to be this way."

She stared down at me. The tears were frozen there, like little tiny shards of ice. "It doesn't?"

"No. It doesn't."

"You mean . . . you mean I can go back?"

I nodded. "You can. You can start over."

She sniffled. "How?"

I said, "All you have to do is make up your mind to do it."

A scowl passed over her pretty face. "But I already made up my mind that that's what I want. All I've wanted since it . . . since it happened . . . was to get my life back."

I shook my head. "No, Heather," I said. "You

misunderstand me. You can never have your life—your *old* life—back. But you can start a new one. That's got to be better than this, than being here all by yourself forever, storming around in a rage, hurting people—"

She shouted, "You said I could get my life back!"

I realized, all in a flash, that I'd lost her. "I didn't mean your old life. I just meant *a* life—"

But it was too late. She was freaking.

I understood now why Bryce's parents had sent him to Antigua. I wished I were there—anywhere, really, if it would get me out of the way of this girl's wrath.

"You told me," Heather screamed, "you told me I could get my life back! You lied to me!"

"Heather, I didn't lie. I just meant that your life—well, your life is over. Heather, you ended it yourself. I know that sucks, but hey, you should have thought of that—"

She cut me off with an unearthly—well, of course—wail. "I won't let you," she shrieked. "I won't let you take over my life!"

"Heather, I told you, I'm not trying to. I have my own life. I don't need yours—"

With the crickets and the birds silent, the sound of the water burbling in the fountain a few yards away had been the only noise in the courtyard—with the exception of Heather's screaming, that is. But the water sounded strange, suddenly. It was making a funny popping noise. I looked toward it, and saw that steam was rising from its surface. I wouldn't have thought that was so strange—it was cold out, and the water temperature might have been warmer than the air around it—if I hadn't seen a great big bubble burst suddenly on the water's surface.

That's when it hit me. She was making the water boil. She was making the water boil with the force of her rage.

"Heather," I said, from my bench. "Heather, listen to me. You've got to calm down. We can't talk when you're—"

"You . . . said . . ." Heather's eyes, I was alarmed to see, had rolled back into her head. "I . . . could . . . start . . . over!"

Okay. It was time to do something. I didn't need the bench beneath me to start shaking so violently that I was nearly thrown from it. I knew it was time to get up.

I did so, fast. Fast so that I wouldn't get hit by the bench. Fast so that I could reach Heather before she noticed, and deck her as hard as I could with a right beneath the chin.

Only to my astonishment, she didn't even seem to feel it. She was too far gone. Way too far gone. Hitting her had no effect whatsoever—except that it really hurt my knuckles. And, of course, it seemed to make her even madder, always a plus when dealing with a severely disturbed individual.

"You," Heather said in a deep voice that was nothing like her normal cheerleader chirp, "are going to be sorry now."

The water in the fountain suddenly reached boiling point. Giant waves of it began sloshing over the side of the basin. The jets, which normally bubbled a mere four feet into the air, suddenly shot up to ten, twenty feet, cascading back down into a bubbling, steaming cauldron. The birds in the treetops took off as one, their wings momentarily blocking out the light from the moon.

I had a funny feeling Heather was serious. What's more, I had a feeling she could do it, too. Without even lifting a finger.

And I had confirmation of that fact when suddenly, Junipero Serra's head was whipped from his statue's body. That's right. It just snapped off as easily as if the solid bronze it was made out of was actually spun candy. Noiselessly, too, she broke it off. The head hung in the air for a moment, its look of sympathetic compassion transformed from the bizarre angle at which it hung over my face into a demonic sneer. Then, as I stood there, transfixed, staring at the way the floodlights winked against the metal ball, I saw it dip suddenly . . .

Then plunge toward me, hurtling so fast it was only a blur in the night sky, like a comet, or a—

I didn't get a chance to think what else it reminded me of because a split second later something heavy hit me in the stomach and sent me sprawling to the dirt, where I lay, looking up at the starry sky. It was so pretty. The night was so black, and the stars so cold and far off and twinkly—

"Get up!" A man's voice sounded harshly in my ear. "I thought you were supposed to be good at this!"

Something exploded in the dirt just an inch from my cheek. I turned my head and saw Junipero Serra's head grinning obscenely at me.

Then Jesse was yanking me to my feet and pulling me toward the breezeway.

# chapter eleven

We made it back into Mr. Walden's classroom. I don't know how, but we did it, the statue's head hurtling after us the whole way, the velocity with which it was traveling causing it to whistle eerily, as if Father Serra were screaming. The head collided with all the force of a cannonball against the heavy wooden door just as we slammed it closed behind us.

"*Jesucrísto,*" Jesse sputtered, as we leaned, panting, with our backs pressed up against the door as if with our sheer weight, we could keep her out—Heather, who could walk through walls if she wanted to." 'I can take care of myself,' you said. 'I'll just have to get rid of her first,' you told me. Right!"

I was trying to catch my breath, think what to do. I had never seen anything like that. Never. "Shut up," I said.

"Cadaver breath." Jesse turned his head to look down at me. His chest was rising and falling. "Do you realize that's what you called me? That hurt, you know, *querida*. It really hurt."

"I told you—" Something heavy was buffeting against the door. I could feel it knocking against my spine. It didn't take a genius to guess it was the founder of a certain mission's head. "—not to call me that."

"Well, I would appreciate if you didn't make disparaging remarks about my—"

"Look," I said. "This door isn't going to hold up forever."

"No," he agreed, just as the metal head managed to smash its way partly through a spot it had weakened in the wood. "May I make a suggestion?"

I was staring, horrified, down at the head, which had turned, halfway in and halfway out of the door, to look up at me with cold, bronze eyes. It's crazy, but I could have sworn it was smiling at me. "Sure," I said.

"Run."

I wasted no time in taking his advice. I ran for

the windowsill and, heedless of the shards of broken glass, swung myself up onto it. It only took a few seconds to open the window again, but that was long enough for Jesse, still pushing against what had begun to sound like a hurricane with all the banging and wailing, to say, "Uh, hurry, please?"

I jumped down into the parking lot. It was kind of funny how, outside the thick adobe walls of the Mission, you couldn't tell at all that there was a severe paranormal disturbance going on inside. The parking lot was still empty, and still quiet, except for the gentle, rhythmic sound of ocean waves. It's just amazing what can be going on beneath people's noses, and they have no idea . . . no idea at all.

"Jesse!" I hissed through the window. "Come on!" I had no idea if Heather might decide to take out her rage with me on an innocent party—or, if she did, whether Jesse had any cool tricks, like the one she'd pulled with the statue's head, of his own. All I knew was that the sooner the both of us got out of her range, the better.

Okay, let me state right now that I am not a coward. I'm really not. But I'm not a fool, either. I think if you recognize that you are up against a force greater than your own, it is perfectly okay to run.

It's not okay to leave others behind, though.

*"Jesse!"* I screamed through the window.

"I thought I told you," said a very irritated voice from behind me, "to run."

I gasped and spun around. Jesse stood there on the asphalt of the parking lot, the moon at his back, casting his face into shadow.

"Oh my God." My heart was beating so fast, I thought it was going to explode. I had never been so scared in all my life. Never.

Maybe that's why I did what I did next, which was reach out and grab the front of Jesse's shirt in both my hands. "Oh my God," I said again. "Jesse, are you all right?"

"Of course I'm all right." He sounded surprised I'd even bother to ask. And I guess it *was* stupid. What could Heather do to Jesse, after all? She couldn't exactly kill him. "Are *you* all right?"

"Me? I'm fine." I turned my head to search the darkened windows of Mr. Walden's classroom. "Do you think she's . . . done?"

"For now," Jesse said.

"How do you know?" I was shocked to find that I was shaking—really shaking—all over. "How do you know she won't come bursting through that wall there and start uprooting all those trees and hurling them at us?"

Jesse shook his head, and I could see that he was smiling. You know, for a guy who died before they invented orthodontia, he had pretty nice teeth. Almost as nice as Bryce's. "She won't."

"How do you *know*?"

"Because she won't. She doesn't know she can. She's too new at all this, Susannah. She doesn't know yet all that she can do."

If that was supposed to make me feel better, it didn't work. The fact that he admitted she *could* uproot trees and start hurling them at me—she was *that* powerful—and only hadn't due to lack of experience, was enough to stop my shaking cold, and drop the handfuls of shirt I held. Not that I didn't think Heather could have followed me if she wanted to. She could, the same way Jesse had followed me down to the Mission. But the thing of it was, Jesse knew he could. He'd been a ghost a lot longer than Heather. She was only just beginning to explore her new powers.

That was the scariest part. She was so new at all of this . . . and already that powerful.

I started pacing around the parking lot like a crazy woman.

"We've got to do something," I said. "We've got to warn Father Dominic—and Bryce. My God, we've got to warn Bryce not to come to school tomorrow. She'll kill him the minute he sets foot on campus—"

"Susannah," Jesse said.

"I guess we could call him. It's one in the morning, but we could call him, and tell him—I don't know what we could tell him. We could tell him there's been a death threat on him or something. That might work. Or—we could *leave* a death threat. Yeah, that's what we could do! We could call his house and I could disguise my voice, and I could be like 'Don't come to school tomorrow, or you'll die.' Maybe he'd listen. Maybe he'd—"

"Susannah," Jesse said again.

"Or we could have Father Dom do it! We could have Father Dom call Bryce and tell him not to come to school, that there's been some kind of accident or something—"

"Susannah." Jesse stepped in front of me just as I turned around to retread the same five feet I'd been pacing for the past few minutes. I came up short, startled by his sudden proximity, my nose practically banging into the place where his shirt collar was open. Jesse seized both my arms quickly, to steady me.

This was not a good thing. I mean, I know a minute ago I had grabbed him—well, not really him, but his shirt. But I don't like being touched under normal circumstances, and I especially don't like being touched by ghosts. And I *especially* don't like being touched by ghosts who have hands as big and as tendony and strong-looking as Jesse's.

"Susannah," he said again, before I could tell him to get his big tendony hands off me. "It's all right. It's not your fault. There was nothing you could do."

I sort of forgot about being mad about his hands. "Nothing I could do? Are you kidding me? I should have kicked that girl back into her grave!"

"No." Jesse shook his head. "She'd have killed you."

"Bull! I totally could have taken her. If she hadn't done that thing with that guy's head—"

"Susannah."

"I mean it, Jesse, I could totally have handled her if she hadn't gotten so mad. I bet if I just wait a little while until she's calmed down and go back in there, I can talk her into—"

"No." He let go of my arms, but only so he could wrap one of his own around my shoulders and start steering me away from the school and toward the Dumpster where I'd parked my bike. "Come on. Let's go home."

"But what about—"

The grip on my shoulders tightened. "No."

"Jesse, you don't understand. This is my *job*. I have to—"

"It's Father Dominic's job, too, no? Let him take it from here. There's no reason why you have to be burdened with all the responsibility yourself."

"Well, yes, there is. I'm the one who screwed up."

"You put the gun to her head and pulled the trigger?"

"Of course not. But I'm the one who got her so mad. Father Dom didn't. I can't ask Father Dom to clean up my messes. That is totally unfair."

"What is totally unfair," Jesse explained—patiently, I guess, for him, "is for anyone to expect a young girl like yourself to do battle with a demon from hell like—"

"She isn't a demon from hell. She's just mad. She's mad because the one guy she thought she could trust turned out to be a—"

"Susannah." Jesse stopped walking suddenly. The only reason I didn't lurch forward and fall flat on my face was that he still kept hold of my shoulder.

For a minute—just a minute—I really thought

. . . well, I thought he was going to kiss me. I'd never been kissed before, but it seemed as if all the necessities for a kiss to happen were there: You know, his arm was around me, there was moonlight, our hearts were racing—oh, yeah, and we'd both just narrowly escaped being killed by a really pissed-off ghost.

Of course, I didn't know how I felt about my first kiss coming from one of the undead, but hey, beggars can't be choosers, and let me tell you something, Jesse was way cuter than any live guy I'd met lately. I'd never seen such a nice-looking ghost. He couldn't, I thought, have been more than twenty when he died. I wondered what had killed him. It's usually hard to tell with ghosts, since their spirits tend to take on the shape their body was in just before they stopped functioning. My dad, for instance, doesn't look any different when he appears to me now than he did the day before he went out for that fatal jog around Prospect Park ten years ago.

I could only assume Jesse had died at someone else's hands since he looked pretty damned healthy to me. Chances were he'd been a victim of one of those bullet holes downstairs. Nice of Andy to frame it for posterity's sake.

And now this extremely nice-looking ghost

looked as if he were going to kiss me. Well, who was I to stop him?

So I sort of leaned my head back and looked out at him from underneath my eyelids, and sort of let my mouth get all relaxed, you know? And that's when I noticed his attention wasn't focused anywhere near my lips, but way below them. And not my chest, either, which would have been an okay second.

"You're bleeding," he said.

Well, that pretty much spoiled the moment. My eyes popped wide open at *that* remark.

"I am not," I said automatically since I didn't feel any pain. Then I looked down. There were smallish stains flowering on the pavement below my feet. You couldn't tell what color they were because it was so dark. In the moonlight, they looked black. There were similar dark stains, I saw with horror, on the front of Jesse's shirt.

But they were definitely coming from me. I checked myself out, and found that I'd managed to open what was probably one of the smaller, but still fairly important, veins in my wrist. I'd peeled off my gloves and stuffed them in my pockets while I'd been talking to Heather, and in my haste to escape during her fit of rage, I'd forgotten to put them back on. I'd probably sliced myself on the broken glass still littering the windowsill in Mr. Walden's classroom when I'd vaulted up onto it during my escape. Which just proved my theory that it's always on the way out that you get stuck.

"Oh," I said, watching the blood ooze out. I couldn't think of anything else to say but, "What a mess. I'm sorry about your shirt."

"It's nothing." Jesse reached into one of the pockets of his dark, narrow-fitting trousers and pulled out something white and soft that he wrapped around my wrist a few times, then tied into place like a tourniquet, only not as tight. He didn't say anything as he did this, concentrating on what he was doing. I have to say this was the first time a ghost had ever performed first aid on me. Not quite as interesting as a kiss would have been, but not entirely boring, either.

"There," he said when he was finished. "Does that hurt?"

"No," I said, since it didn't. It wouldn't start hurting, I knew from experience, for a few hours. I cleared my throat. "Thanks."

"It's nothing," he said.

"No," I said. Suddenly, ridiculously, I felt like crying. Really. And I never cry. "I mean it. Thanks. Thanks for coming out here to help me.

You shouldn't have done it. I mean, I'm glad you did. And . . . well, thanks. That's all."

He looked embarrassed. Well, I suppose that was natural, me going all mushy on him the way I had just then. But I couldn't help it. I mean, I still couldn't really believe it. No ghost had ever been so nice to me. Oh, my dad tried, I guess. But he wasn't exactly what you'd call reliable about it. I could never really count on him, especially in a crisis.

But Jesse. Jesse had come through for me. And I hadn't even asked him to. In fact, I'd been pretty unpleasant to him, overall.

"Never mind," was all he said, though. And then he added, "Let's go home."

# chapter *twelve*

Let's go home.

It had a very cozy feel to it, that "Let's go home."

Except, of course, that the house we shared didn't quite feel like home to me yet. How could it? I'd only lived there a few days.

And, of course, *he* shouldn't have been living there at all.

Still, ghost or not, he'd saved my life. There was no denying that. He'd probably only done it to get on my good side so I wouldn't kick him out of the house entirely.

But regardless of why he'd done it, it had still been pretty nice of him. Nobody had ever volunteered to help me before—mostly because, of course, nobody knew I needed help. Even Gina, who'd been there when Madame Zara had first pronounced me a mediator, never knew why it was I would show up to school so groggy-eyed, or where it was I went when I cut class—which I did all too frequently. And I couldn't exactly explain. Not that Gina would have thought I was crazy or anything, but she'd have told someone—you can't keep something like this secret unless it's happening to you—who'd have told someone else, and eventually, somewhere along the line, I knew someone would have told my mother.

And my mother would have freaked. That is, naturally, what mothers do, and mine is no exception. She'd already stuck me in therapy where I was forced to sit and invent elaborate lies in the hopes of explaining my antisocial behavior. I did not need to spend any time in a mental institution, which was undoubtedly where I'd have ended up if my mother had ever found out the truth.

So, yeah, I was grateful to have Jesse along, even though he sort of made me nervous. After the debacle at the Mission, he walked me home, which was gentlemanly and all. He even, in deference to my injury, insisted on pushing the bike.

I suppose if anybody had looked out the window of any of the houses we were passing, they would have thought their eyes were playing tricks on them: They'd have seen me plodding along with this bike rolling effortlessly beside me—*only my hands weren't touching the bike.*

Good thing people on the West Coast go to bed so early.

The whole way home, I obsessed over what I'd done wrong in my dealings with Heather. I didn't do it out loud—I figured I'd done enough of that; I didn't want to sound like a broken record or player piano, or whatever it was they had back in Jesse's day. But it was all I could think about. Never, not in all my years of mediating, had I ever encountered such a violent, irrational spirit. I simply did not know what to do. And I knew I had to figure it out, and quick; I only had a few hours before school started and Bryce walked straight into what was, for him, a deathtrap.

I don't know if Jesse figured out why I was so quiet, or if he was thinking about Heather, too, or what. All I know was that suddenly, he broke the silence we'd been walking in and went, "'Heav'n has no rage like love to hatred turn'd, nor hell a fury like a woman scorned.'"

I looked at him. "Are you speaking from experience?"

I saw him smile a little in the moonlight. "Actually," he said, "I am quoting William Congreve."

"Oh." I thought about that. "But you know, sometimes the woman scorned has every right to be mad."

"Are *you* speaking from experience?" he wanted to know.

I snorted. "Not hardly." A guy has to like you before he can scorn you. But I didn't say that out loud. No way would I ever say something like that out loud. I mean, not that I *cared* what Jesse thought about me. Why should I care what some dead cowboy thought of me?

But I wasn't about to admit to him that I'd never had a boyfriend. You just don't go around saying things like that to totally hot guys, even if they're dead.

"But we don't know what went on between Heather and Bryce—not really. I mean, she could have every right to feel resentful."

"Toward him, I suppose she does," Jesse said, though he sounded grudging about admitting it. "But not toward *you.* She had no right to try to hurt *you.*"

He sounded so mad about it that I thought it was probably better to change the subject. I mean, I guess I should have been mad about Heather trying to kill me, but you know, I'm sort of used to dealing with irrational people. Well, okay, not quite as irrational as Heather, but you know what I mean. And one thing I've learned is, you can't take it personally. Yeah, she'd tried to kill me, but I wasn't really sure she knew any better. Who knew what kind of parents she had, after all? Maybe they went around murdering anybody who made them mad. . . .

Although somehow, after having seen that add-a-pearl necklace, I sort of doubted that.

Thinking about murder made me wonder what had gotten Jesse so hot under the collar about it. Then I realized that he'd probably been murdered. Either that or he'd killed himself. But I didn't think he was really the suicide type. I supposed he could have died of some sort of wasting disease. . . .

It probably wasn't very tactful of me—but then, nobody's ever accused me of tact—but I went ahead and just asked him as we were climbing the long gravel driveway to the house, "Hey. How'd you die, anyway?"

Jesse didn't say anything right away. I'd probably offended him. Ghosts don't really like talking about how they died, I've noticed. Sometimes they can't even remember. Car crash victims usually haven't the slightest clue what happened to them. That's why I always see them wandering around looking for the other people who were in the car with them. I have to go up and explain to them what happened, and then try to figure out where the people are that they're looking for. This is a major pain, too, let me tell you. I have to go all the way to the precinct that took the accident report and pretend I'm doing a school report or whatever and record the names of the victims, then follow up on what happened to them.

I tell you, sometimes I feel like my work never ends.

Anyway, Jesse was quiet for a while, and I figured he wasn't going to tell me. He was looking straight ahead, up at the house—the house where he'd died, the house he was destined to haunt until . . . well, until he resolved whatever it was that was holding him to this world.

The moon was still out, pretty high in the sky now, and I could see Jesse's face almost as if it were day. He didn't look a whole lot different than usual. His mouth, which was on the thin-but-wide side, was kind of frowning, which, as near as I could tell, was what it usually did. And underneath those glossy black eyebrows, his thickly lashed eyes revealed about as much as a mirror—that is, I could probably have seen my reflection in them, but I could read nothing about what he might be thinking.

"Um," I said. "You know what? Never mind. If you don't want to tell me, you don't have to—"

"No," he said. "It's all right."

"I was just kinda curious, that's all," I said. "But if it's too personal . . ."

"It isn't too personal." We had reached the house by then. He wheeled the bike to where it was supposed to go, and leaned it up against the carport wall. He was deep in the shadows when he said, "You know this house wasn't always a family home."

I went, "Oh, really?" Like this was the first I'd heard of it.

"Yes. It was once a hotel. Well, more like a boardinghouse, really, than a hotel."

I asked brightly, "And you were staying here as a guest?"

"Yes." He came out from the shade of the carport, but he wasn't looking at me when he spoke next. He was squinting out toward the sea.

"And . . ." I tried to prompt him. "Something

happened while you were staying here?"

"Yes." He looked at me then. He looked at me for a long time. Then he said, "But it's a long story, and you must be very tired. Go to bed. In the morning we will decide what to do about Heather."

Talk about unfair!

"Wait a minute," I said. "I am not going anywhere until you finish that story."

He shook his head. "No. It's too late. I'll tell you some other time."

"Jeez!" I sounded like a little kid whose mom had told him to go to bed early, but I didn't care. I was mad. "You can't just start a story and then not finish it. You have to—"

Jesse was laughing at me now. "Go to bed, Susannah," he said, coming up and giving me a gentle push toward the front steps. "You have had enough scaring for one night."

"But you—"

"Some other time," he said. He had steered me in the direction of the porch, and now I stood on the lowest step, looking back at him as he laughed at me.

"Do you promise?"

I saw his teeth flash white in the moonlight. "I promise. Good night, *querida.*"

"I told you," I grumbled, stomping up the steps, "not to call me that."

It was nearly 3:00 in the morning, though, and I could only summon up token indignation. I was still on New York time, remember, three hours ahead. It had been hard enough getting up in time for school when I'd had a full eight hours of sleep. How hard was it going to be after only having had four?

I slipped into the house as quietly as I could. Fortunately, everybody except the dog was dead asleep. The dog looked up from the couch on which he was reclining and wagged his tail when he saw it was me. Some watchdog. Plus my mom didn't want him sleeping on her white couch. But I wasn't about to make an enemy out of Max by shooing him off. If allowing him to sleep on the couch was all that was necessary to keep him from alerting the household that I'd been out, then it was well worth it.

I slogged up the stairs, wondering the whole time what I was going to do about Heather. I guessed I was going to have to wake up early and call over to the school, and warn Father Dom to meet Bryce the minute he set foot on campus and send him home. Even, I decided, if we had to resort to head lice, I wouldn't object. All that mattered, in the long run, was that Heather was kept from her goal.

Still, the thought of waking up early to do anything—even save the life of my date for Saturday night—was not very appealing. Now that the adrenaline rush was gone, I realized I was dead tired. I staggered into the bathroom to change into my pj's—hey, I was pretty sure Jesse wasn't spying on me, but he still hadn't told me how he'd died, so I wasn't taking any chances. He could have been hanged, you know, for Peeping Tomism, which I believed happened occasionally a hundred and fifty years ago.

It wasn't until I was changing the bandage on the cut on my wrist that I happened to take a look at the thing he'd wrapped around it.

It was a handkerchief. Everybody carried one in the olden days because there was no such thing as Kleenex. People were pretty fussy about them, too, sewing their initials onto them so they didn't get mixed up in the wash with other people's hankies.

Only Jesse's handkerchief didn't have his initials on it, I noticed after I'd rinsed it in the sink then wrung out my blood as best I could. It was a big linen square, white—well, kind of pink now—with an edging all around it of this delicate white lace. Kind of femme for a guy. I might have been a little concerned about Jesse's sexual orientation if I hadn't noticed the initials sewn in one corner. The stitches were tiny, white thread on white material, but the letters themselves were huge, in flowery script: MDS. That was right. MDS. No J to be found.

Weird. Very weird.

I hung the cloth up to dry. I didn't have to worry about anybody seeing it. In the first place, nobody used my bathroom but me, and in the second place, nobody would be able to see it anymore than they could see Jesse. It would be there tomorrow. Maybe I wouldn't give it back to him without demanding some sort of explanation as to those letters. MDS.

It wasn't until I was falling asleep that I realized MDS must have been a girl. Why else would there have been all that lace? And that curlicue script? Had Jesse died not in a gunfight, as I'd originally assumed, but in some sort of lovers' quarrel?

I don't know why the thought disturbed me so much, but it did. It kept me awake for about three whole minutes. Then I rolled over, missed my old bed very briefly, and fell asleep.

# chapter thirteen

My intention, of course, had been to wake up early and call Father Dominic to warn him about Heather. But intentions are only as good as the people who hold them, and I guess I must be worthless because I didn't wake up until my mother shook me awake, and by then it was 7:30, and my ride was leaving without me.

Or so they thought. There was a huge delay when Sleepy discovered he'd lost the keys to the Rambler, so I was able to drag myself out of bed and into some kind of outfit—I had no idea what. I came staggering down the stairs, feeling like somebody had hit me on the head a few times with a bag of rocks just as Doc was telling everybody that Sister Ernestine had warned him if he missed another Assembly, he'd be held back a year.

That's when I remembered the keys to the Rambler were still in the pocket of my leather jacket where I'd left them the night before.

I slunk back up the stairs and pretended to find the keys on the landing. There was some jubilation over this, but mostly a lot of grumbling, since Sleepy swore he'd left them hanging on the key hook in the kitchen and couldn't figure out how they'd gotten to the landing. Dopey said, "It was probably Dave's ghost," and leered at Doc, who looked embarrassed.

Then we all piled into the car and took off.

We were late, of course. Assembly at the Junipero Serra Mission Academy begins promptly at 8:00. We got there at around two after. What happens at Assembly is, they make everybody stand outside in these lines separated by sex, boys on one side, girls on the other—like we're Quakers or something—for fifteen minutes before school officially starts, so they can take attendance and read announcements and stuff. By the time we got there, of course, Assembly had already started. I had intended to duck right past and head straight to Father Dominic's office, but of course, I never got the chance. Sister Ernestine caught us traipsing in late, and gave each of us the evil eye until we slunk into our various lines. I didn't much care what Sister Ernestine jotted down in her little black book about me, but I could see that getting to the principal's office was going to be impossible, due to the yellow caution tape strung up across every single archway that led to the courtyard—and, of course, all the cops.

I guess what had happened was, all the priests and nuns and stuff had gotten up for matins, which is what they call the first mass of the morning, and they'd all walked outside and seen the statue of their church's founder with his head cut off, and the fountain with hardly any water left in it, and the bench where I'd been sitting all twisted and tipped over, and the door to Mr. Walden's classroom in smithereens.

Understandably, I guess, they freaked out and called the cops. People in uniform were crawling all over the place, taking fingerprints and measuring stuff, like the distance Junipero Serra's head had traveled from his body, and the velocity it had to have traveled to make that many holes in a door that was made of three-inch-thick wood, and that kind of thing. I saw a guy in a dark blue windbreaker with the letters

CBTSPD—Carmel-by-the-Sea Police Department?—on the back, conferring with Father Dominic, who looked really, really tired. I couldn't catch his eye, and supposed I'd have to wait until after Assembly to sneak away and apologize to him.

At Assembly, Sister Ernestine, the vice principal, told us vandals had done it. Vandals had broken in through Mr. Walden's classroom, and wreaked havoc all over the school. What was fortunate, we were told, was that the solid gold chalice and salver used for the sacramental wine and hosts had not been stolen, but were left sitting in their little cupboard behind the church altar. The vandals had rudely beheaded our school founder, but left the really valuable stuff alone. We were told that if any of us knew anything about this horrible violation, we were to come forward immediately. And that if we were uncomfortable coming forward personally, we could do it anonymously—Monsignor Constantine would be hearing confessions all morning.

As if! Hey, it hadn't been *my* fault Heather had gone berserk. Well, not really, anyway. If anybody should be going to confession, it was *her*.

As I stood in line—behind CeeCee, who couldn't hide her delight over what had happened; you could practically see the headline forming in her mind: *Father Serra Loses His Head Over Vandals*—I craned my neck, trying to see over to the seniors. Was Bryce there? I couldn't see him. Maybe Father Dom had gotten to him already, and sent him home. He had to have recognized that the mess in the courtyard was the result of spiritual, not human, agitation, and had acted accordingly. I hoped, for Bryce's sake, that Father Dom hadn't resorted to the head lice.

Okay, I hoped it for my sake, I admit it. I really wanted our date on Saturday to go well, and not be canceled due to head lice. Is that such a crime? A girl can't spend *all* her time battling psychic disturbances. She needs a little romance, too.

But of course, the minute Assembly was over and I tried to ditch homeroom and hightail it to Father Dom's office, Sister Ernestine caught me and said, just as I was about to duck under some of the yellow caution tape, "Excuse me, Miss Simon. Perhaps back in New York it is perfectly all right to ignore police warnings, but here in California it is considered highly ill-advised."

I straightened. I had nearly made it, too. I thought some uncharitable things about Sister Ernestine, but managed to say, civilly enough, "Oh, Sister, I'm so sorry. You see, I just need to get to Father Dominic's office."

"Father Dominic," Sister Ernestine said coldly, "is extremely busy this morning. He happens to be consulting with the police over last night's unfortunate incident. He won't be available until after lunch at the earliest."

I know it's probably wrong to fantasize about giving a nun a karate chop in the neck, but I couldn't help it. She was making me mad.

"Listen, Sister," I said. "Father Dominic asked me to come see him this morning. I've got some, um, transcripts from my old school that he wanted to see. I had to have them FedExed all the way from New York, and they just got here, so—"

I thought that was pretty quick thinking on my part, about the transcripts and the FedEx and all, but then Sister Ernestine held out her hand and went, "Give them to me, and I'll be happy to deliver them to the Father."

Damn!

"Uh," I said, backing away. "Never mind. I guess I'll just . . . I'll see him after lunch, then."

Sister Ernestine gave me a kind of aha-I-thought-so look, then turned her attention to some innocent kid who'd made the mistake of coming to school in a pair of Levi's, a blatant violation of the dress code. The kid wailed, "They were my only clean pants!" but Sister Ernestine didn't care. She stood there—unfortunately still guarding the only route to the principal's office—and wrote the kid up on the spot.

I had no choice but to go to class. I mean, what was there to tell Father Dominic, anyway, that he didn't already know? I'm sure he knew it was Heather who'd wrecked the school, and me who'd broken Mr. Walden's window. He probably wasn't going to be all that happy with me anyway, so why was I even bothering? What I ought to have been doing was trying as much as possible to stay out of his way.

Except . . . except what about Heather?

As near as I could tell, she was still recuperating from her explosive rage the night before. I saw no sign of her as I made my way to Mr. Walden's classroom for first period, which was good: It meant Father D. and I would have time to draw up some kind of plan before she struck again.

As I sat there in class trying to convince myself that everything was going to be all right, I couldn't help feeling kind of bad for poor Mr. Walden. He was taking having the door to his classroom obliterated pretty well. He didn't even seem to mind the broken window so much. Of course, everybody in school was buzzing about what had happened. People were saying that it had been a prank, the severing of Junipero Serra's head. A senior prank. One year, CeeCee told me, the seniors had strapped pillows to the clappers of the church bells, so that when they rang, all that came out was a muffled sort of splatting sound. I guess people suspected this was the same sort of thing.

If only they had known the truth. Heather's seat, next to Kelly Prescott, remained conspicuously vacant, while her locker—now assigned to me—was still unopenable thanks to the dent her body had made when I'd thrown her against it.

It was sort of ironic that as I was sitting there thinking this, Kelly Prescott raised her hand and, when Mr. Walden called on her, asked if he didn't think it was unfair, Monsignor Constantine declaring that no memorial service would be held for Heather.

Mr. Walden leaned back in his seat and put both his feet up on his desk. Then he said, "Don't look at me. I just work here."

"Well," Kelly said, "don't you think it's unfair?" She turned to the rest of the class, her big, mascara-rimmed eyes appealing. "Heather Chambers went here for ten years. It's inexcusable that she shouldn't be memorialized in her own school. And, frankly, I think what happened yesterday was a sign."

Mr. Walden looked vastly amused. "A sign, Kelly?"

"That's right. I believe what happened here last night—and even that piece of the breezeway nearly killing Bryce—are all connected. I don't believe Father Serra's statue was desecrated by vandals at all, but by angels. Angels who are angry about Monsignor Constantine not allowing Heather's parents to have her funeral here."

This caused a good deal of buzzing in the classroom. People looked nervously at Heather's empty chair. Normally, I don't talk much in school, but I couldn't let this one go by. I said, "So you're saying you think it was an angel who broke this window behind me, Kelly?"

Kelly had to twist around in her seat to see me. "Well," she said. "It could have been. . . ."

"Right. And you think it was angels who broke down Mr. Walden's door, and cut off that statue's head, and wrecked the courtyard?"

Kelly stuck out her chin. "Yes," she said. "I do. Angels angered over Monsignor Constantine's decision not to allow us to memorialize Heather."

I shook my head. "Bull," I said.

Kelly raised her eyebrows. "I beg your pardon?"

"I said bull, Kelly. I think your theory is full of bull."

Kelly turned a very interesting shade of red. I think she was probably regretting inviting me to her pool party. "You don't know it wasn't angels, Suze," she said acidly.

"Actually, I do. Because to the best of my knowledge, angels don't bleed, and there was blood all over the carpeting back here from where the vandal hurt himself breaking in. That's why the police cut up chunks of the rug and took them away."

Kelly wasn't the only one who gasped. Everybody kind of freaked out. I probably shouldn't have pointed out the blood—especially since it was mine—but hey, I couldn't let her go around saying it was all because of angels. Angels, my butt. What did she think this was, anyway, *Highway to Heaven*?

"Okay," Mr. Walden said. "On that note, everybody, it's time for second period. Susannah, could I see you a minute?"

CeeCee turned around to waggle her white eyebrows at me. "You're in for it now, sucker," she hissed.

But she had no idea how true her words were. All anybody would have to do was take a look at the Band-Aids all over my wrist, and they'd know I had firsthand knowledge of where that blood had come from.

On the other hand, they had no reason to suspect me, did they?

I approached Mr. Walden's desk, my heart in my throat. *He's going to turn you in*, I thought, frantically. *You are so busted, Simon.*

But all Mr. Walden wanted to do was compliment me on my use of footnotes in my essay on the battle of Bladensburg, which he had noticed as I handed it in.

"Uh," I said. "It was really no big deal, Mr. Walden."

"Yes, but footnotes—" He sighed. "I haven't seen footnotes used correctly since I taught an adult education class over at the community college. Really, you did a great job."

I muttered a modest thank-you. I didn't want to admit that the reason I knew so much about the battle of Bladensburg was that I'd once helped a veteran of that battle direct a couple of his ancestors to a long-buried bag of money he'd dropped during it. It's funny the things that hold people back from getting on with their life . . . or their death, I should say.

I was about to tell Mr. Walden that while I'd have loved, under ordinary circumstances, to stick around and chat about famous American battles, I really had to go—I was going to see if Sister Ernestine was still guarding the way to Father Dom's office—when Mr. Walden stopped me cold with these few words: "It's funny about Kelly bringing up Heather Chambers that way, actually, Susannah."

I eyed him warily. "Oh? How so?"

"Well, I don't know if you're aware of this, but Heather was the sophomore class vice president, and now that she's gone, we've been collecting nominations for a new VP. Well, believe it or not, you've been nominated. Twelve times so far."

My eyes must have bugged out of my head. I forgot all about how I had to go and see Father Dominic. "*Twelve* times?"

"Yes, I know, it's unusual, isn't it?"

I couldn't believe it. "But I've only been going here one day!"

"Well, you've made quite an impression. I myself would guess that you didn't exactly make any enemies yesterday when you offered to break Debbie Mancuso's fingers after school. She is not one of the better-liked girls in the class."

I stared at him. So Mr. Walden *had* overheard my little threat. The fact that he had and not sent me straight to detention made me appreciate him in a way I'd never appreciated a teacher before.

"Oh, and I guess your pushing Bryce Martinson out of the way of that flying chunk of wood—that probably didn't hurt much, either," he added.

"Wow," I said. I guess I probably don't need to point out that at my old school, I wouldn't exactly have won any popularity contests. I never even bothered going out for cheerleading or running for homecoming queen. Besides the fact that at my old school cheerleading was considered a stupid waste of time and in Brooklyn it isn't exactly a compliment to be called a queen, I never would have made either one. And no one—*no one*—had ever nominated me before for anything.

I was way too flattered to follow my initial instinct, which was to say, "Thanks, but no thanks," and run.

"Well," I said instead, "what does the vice president of the sophomore class have to do?"

Mr. Walden shrugged. "Help the president determine how to spend the class budget, mostly. It's not much, just a little over three thousand dollars. Kelly and Heather were planning on using the money to hold a dance over at the Carmel Inn, but—"

*"Three thousand dollars?"* My mouth was probably hanging open, but I didn't care.

"Yes, I know it's not much—"

"And we can spend it any way we want?" My mind was spinning. "Like, if we wanted to have a bunch of cookouts down at the beach, we could do that?"

Mr. Walden looked down at me curiously. "Sure. You have to have the approval of the rest of the class, though. I have a feeling there might be some noises from the administration about using the class money to mend the statue of Father Serra, but—"

But whatever Mr. Walden had been about to say, he didn't get a chance to finish. CeeCee came running back into the classroom, her purple eyes wide behind the tinted prescription lenses of her glasses.

"Come quick!" she yelled. "There's been an accident! Father Dominic and Bryce Martinson—"

I whirled around, fast. "What?" I demanded way more sharply than I needed to. "What about them?"

"I think they're dead!"

# chapter fourteen

I ran so fast that later, Sister Mary Claire, the track coach, asked me if I'd like to try out for the team.

But CeeCee was wrong on all three counts. Father Dominic wasn't dead. Neither was Bryce.

And there'd been nothing accidental about it.

As near as anyone could figure out, what happened was this: Bryce went into the principal's office for something—nobody knew what. A late pass, maybe, since he'd missed Assembly—but not, as I'd hoped, because Father Dom had got hold of him. Bryce had been standing in front of the secretary's desk beneath the giant crucifix Adam had told me would weep tears of blood if a virgin ever graduated from the Mission Academy (the secretary hadn't been there, she'd been out serving coffee to the cops who were still hanging around the courtyard) when the six-foot-tall cross suddenly came loose from the wall. Father Dominic opened his office door just in time to see it falling forward, where it surely would have crushed Bryce's skull. But because Father Dominic shoved him to safety, it succeeded only in delivering a glancing blow that crushed Bryce's collarbone.

Unfortunately, Father Dominic ended up taking the weight of the falling cross himself. It pinned him to the office floor, smashing most of his ribs and breaking one of his legs.

Mr. Walden and a bunch of the sisters tried to get us to go to class instead of crowding the breezeway, watching for Father Dom and Bryce to emerge from the principal's office. Some people went when Sister Ernestine threatened everyone with detention, but not me. I didn't care if I got detention. I had to make sure they were all right. Sister Ernestine said something very nasty about how maybe Miss Simon didn't realize how unpleasant detention at the Mission Academy could be. I assured Sister Ernestine that if she was threatening corporal punishment, I would tell my mother, who was a local news anchorwoman and would be over here with a TV camera so fast, nobody would have time to say so much as a single Hail Mary.

Sister Ernestine was pretty quiet after that.

It was shortly after this that I found Doc pressed up pretty close to me. I looked down and said, "What are *you* doing here?" since the little kids are supposed to stay way on the other side of the school.

"I want to see if he's all right." Doc's freckles were standing out, he was so pale.

"You're going to get in trouble," I warned him. Sister Ernestine was busily writing people up.

"I don't care," Doc said. "I want to see."

I shrugged. He was a funny kid, that Doc. He wasn't anything like his big brothers, and it wasn't because of his red hair, either. I remembered Dopey's teasing comment about the car keys and "Dave's ghost," and wondered how much, if anything, Doc knew about what had been going on lately at his school.

Finally, after what seemed like hours, they came out. Bryce was first, strapped onto a stretcher and moaning, I'm sorry to say, like a bit of a baby. I've had plenty of broken and dislocated bones, and believe me it hurts, but not enough to lie there moaning. Usually when I get hurt, I don't even notice. Like last night, for instance. When I'm *really* hurt all I can do is laugh because it hurts so much that it's actually funny.

Okay, I have to admit I sort of stopped liking Bryce so much when I saw him acting like such a baby. . . .

Especially when I saw Father Dom, who the paramedics wheeled out next. He was unconscious, his white hair sort of flopped over in a sad way, a jagged cut, partially covered by gauze, over his right eye. I hadn't eaten any breakfast in my haste to get to school, and I have to admit the sight of poor Father Dominic with his eyes closed and his glasses gone, made me feel a little woozy. In fact, I might have swayed a little on my feet, and probably would have fallen over if Doc hadn't grabbed my hand and said confidently, "I know. The sight of blood makes me sick, too."

But it wasn't the sight of Father Dom's blood seeping through the bandage on his head that had made me sick. It was the realization that I had failed. I had failed miserably. It was only dumb blind luck that Heather hadn't succeeded in killing them both. It was only because of Father Dom's quick thinking that he and Bryce were alive. It was no thanks to me. No thanks to me whatsoever.

Because if I had handled things better the night before it wouldn't have happened. It wouldn't have happened at all.

That's when I got mad. I mean *really* mad.

Suddenly, I knew what I had to do. I looked down at Doc. "Is there a computer here at school? One with Internet access?"

"Sure," Doc said, looking surprised. "In the library. Why?"

I dropped his hand. "Never mind. Go back to class."

"Suze—"

"Anyone who isn't in his or her classroom in one minute," Sister Ernestine said imperiously, "will be suspended indefinitely!"

Doc tugged on my sleeve.

"What's going on?" he wanted to know. "Why do you need a computer?"

"Nothing," I said. Behind the wrought-iron gate that led to the parking lot, the paramedics slammed the doors to the ambulances in which they'd loaded Father Dom and Bryce. A second later, they were pulling away in a whine of sirens and a flurry of flashing lights. "Just . . . it's stuff you wouldn't understand, David. It isn't scientific."

Doc said, with no small amount of indignation, "I can understand lots of stuff that isn't scientific.

Music, for instance. I've taught myself to play Chopin on my electronic keyboard back home. That isn't scientific. The appreciation of music is purely emotional as is the appreciation of art. I can understand art and music. So come on, Suze," he said. "You can tell me. Does it have anything to do with . . . what we were talking about the other night?"

I turned to gaze down at him in surprise. He shrugged. "It was a logical conclusion. I made a cursory examination of the statue—cursory because I was unable to approach it as closely as I would have liked thanks to the crime scene tape and evidence team—and was unable to discern any saw marks or other indications of how the head was severed. There is no possible way bronze can be cut that cleanly without the use of some sort of heavy machinery, but such machinery would never fit through—"

"Mr. Ackerman!" Sister Ernestine sounded like she meant business. "Would you like to be written up?"

David looked irritated. "No," he said.

"No, what?"

"No, Sister." He looked back at me, apologetically. "I guess I better go. But can we talk more about this tonight at home? I found out some stuff about—well, what you asked me. You know." He widened his eyes meaningfully. "About the house."

"Oh," I said. "Great. Okay."

"Mr. Ackerman!"

David turned to look at the nun. "Hold on a minute, okay, Sister? I'm trying to have a conversation here."

All of the blood left the middle-aged woman's face. It was incredible.

She reacted as childishly as if she were the twelve-year-old, and not David.

"Come with me, young man," she said, seizing hold of David's ear. "I can see your new stepsister has put some pretty big-city ideas into your head about how a boy speaks to his elders—"

David let out a noise like a wounded animal, but went along with the woman, hunched up like a shrimp, he was in so much pain. I swear I wouldn't have done anything—anything at all—if I hadn't suddenly noticed Heather standing just inside the gate, laughing her head off.

"Oh, God," she cried, gasping a little, she was laughing so hard. "If you could have seen your face when you heard Bryce was dead! I swear! It was the funniest thing I've ever seen!" She stopped laughing long enough to toss her long hair and say, "You know what? I think I'm going to clobber a few more people with stuff today. Maybe I'll start with that little guy over there—"

I stepped toward her. "You lay one hand on my brother, and I'll stuff you right back into that grave you crawled out of."

Heather only laughed, but Sister Ernestine, who I realized belatedly thought I was talking to her, let go of David so fast you'd have thought the kid had suddenly caught on fire.

*"What did you say?"*

Sister Ernestine was turning sort of purple. Behind her, Heather laughed delightedly. "Oh, now you've done it. Detention for a week!"

And just like that, she disappeared, leaving behind yet another mess for me to clean up.

As much to my surprise as, I think, her own, Sister Ernestine could only stare at me. David stood there rubbing his ear and looking bewildered. I said as quickly as I could, "We'll go back to our classrooms now. We were only concerned about Father Dominic, and wanted to see him off. Thanks, Sister."

Sister Ernestine continued to stare at me. She didn't say anything. She was a big lady, not quite as tall as me in my two-inch heels—I was wearing black Batgirl boots—but much wider, with exceptionally large breasts. Between them dangled a silver cross. Sister Ernestine fingered this cross unconsciously as she stared at me. Later, Adam, who'd watched the entire event unfold, would say that Sister Ernestine was holding up the cross as if to protect herself from me. That is untrue. She merely touched the cross as if uncertain it was still there. Which it was. It most certainly was.

I guess that was when David stopped being Doc to me, and started being David.

"Don't worry," I told him, just before we parted ways, because he looked so worried and cute and all with his red hair and freckles and sticky-outy ears. I reached out and rumpled some of that red hair. "Everything will be all right."

David looked up at me. "How do you *know*?" he asked.

I took my hand away.

Because, of course, the truth was I didn't. Know everything was going to be all right, I mean. Far from it, as a matter of fact.

# chapter *fifteen*

Lunch was almost over by the time I cornered Adam. I had spent almost the entire period in the library staring into a computer monitor. I still hadn't eaten, but the truth was, I wasn't hungry at all.

"Hey," I said, sitting down next to him and crossing my legs so that my black skirt hiked up just the littlest bit. "Did you drive to school this morning?"

Adam pounded on his chest. He'd started choking on a Frito the minute I'd sat down. When he finally got it down, he said proudly, "I sure did. Now that I got my license, I am a driving machine. You should've come out with us last night, Suze. We had a blast. After we went to the Coffee Clutch, we took a spin along Seventeen Mile Drive. Have you ever done that? Man, with last night's moon, the ocean was so beautiful—"

"Would you mind taking me somewhere after school?"

Adam stood up fast, scaring two fat seagulls that had been sitting near the bench he was sharing with CeeCee. "Are you kidding me? Where do you want to go? You name it, Suze, I'll take you there. Vegas? You want to go to Vegas? No problem. I mean, I'm sixteen, you're sixteen. We can get married there easy. My parents'll let us live with them, no problem. You don't mind sharing my room, do you? I swear I'll pick up after myself from now on—"

"Adam," CeeCee said. "Don't be such a spaz. I highly doubt she wants to marry you."

"I don't think it's a good idea to marry anyone until my divorce from my first husband is finalized," I said gravely. "What I want to do is go to the hospital and see Bryce."

Adam's shoulders slumped. "Oh," he said. There was no missing the dejection in his voice. "Is that all?"

I realized I'd said the wrong thing. Still, I couldn't unsay it. Fortunately, CeeCee helped me out by saying thoughtfully, "You know, a story about Bryce and Father Dominic bravely battling back from their wounds wouldn't be a bad idea for the paper. Would you mind if I tagged along, Suze?"

"Not at all." A lie, of course. With CeeCee along, it might be difficult to accomplish what I wanted without a lot of explaining. . . .

But what choice did I have? None.

Once I'd secured my ride, I started looking for Sleepy. I found him dozing with his back to the monkey bars. I nudged him awake with the toe of my boot. When he squinted up at me through his sunglasses, I told him not to wait for me after school, that I'd found my own ride. He grunted, and went back to sleep.

Then I went and found a pay phone. It's weird when you don't know your own mother's phone number. I mean, I still knew our number back in Brooklyn, but I didn't have the slightest idea what my new phone number was. Good thing I'd written it in my date book. I consulted the A's—for Ackerman—and found my new number, and dialed it. I knew no one was home, but I wanted to cover all my bases. I told the answering machine that I might be late getting back from school since I was going out with a couple of new friends. My mother, I knew, would be delighted when she got back from the station and heard it. She'd always worried, back in Brooklyn, that I was antisocial. She'd always go, "Susie, you're such a pretty girl. I just don't understand why no boys ever call you. Maybe if you didn't look so . . . well, tough. How about giving the leather jacket a rest?"

She'd probably have died of joy if she could have been in the parking lot after school and heard Adam as I approached his car.

"Oh, Cee, here she is." Adam flung open the passenger door of his car—which turned out to be one of the new Volkswagen Bugs; I guess Adam's parents weren't hurting for money—and shooed CeeCee into the backseat. "Come on, Suze, you sit right up front with me."

I peered through my sunglasses—as usual, the morning fog had burned away, and now at 3:00 the sun beat down hard from a perfectly clear blue sky—at CeeCee squashed in the backseat. "Um, really," I said. "CeeCee was here first. I'll sit in the back. I don't mind at all."

"I won't hear of it." Adam stood by the door, holding it open for me. "You're the new girl. The new girl gets to sit in the front."

"Yeah," CeeCee said from the depths of the backseat, "until you refuse to sleep with him.

Then he'll relegate you to the backseat, too."

Adam said, in a *Wizard of Oz* voice, "Ignore that man behind the curtain."

I slid into the front seat, and Adam politely closed the door for me.

"Are you serious?" I turned around to ask CeeCee as Adam made his way around the car to the driver's seat.

CeeCee blinked at me from behind her protective lenses. "Do you really think anybody would sleep with *him*?"

I digested that. "I take it," I said, "that's a no, then."

"Damned straight," CeeCee said just as Adam slid behind the wheel.

"Now," the driver said, flexing his fingers experimentally before switching on the ignition. "I'm thinking this whole thing with the statue and Father Dom and Bryce has really stressed us all out. My parents have a hot tub, you know, which is really ideal for stress like the kind we've all been through today, and I suggest that we all go to my place first for a soak. . . ."

"Tell you what," I said. "Let's skip the hot tub this time and just go straight to the hospital. Maybe, if there's time later—"

"*Yes.*" Adam looked heavenward. "There is a god."

CeeCee said, from the backseat, "She said *maybe,* numbskull. God, try to control yourself."

Adam glanced at me as he eased out of his parking space. "Am I coming on too strong?"

"Uh," I said. "Maybe . . ."

"The thing is, it's been so long since even a remotely interesting girl has shown up around here." Adam, I saw with some relief, was a very careful driver—not like Sleepy, who seemed to think stop signs actually said PAUSE. "I mean, I've been surrounded by Kelly Prescotts and Debbie Mancusos for sixteen years. It's such a relief to have a Susannah Simon around for a change. You *decimated* Kelly this morning when you went, 'Hmm, do angels leave blood stains? I don't *think* so.'"

Adam went on in this vein for the rest of the trip to the hospital. I wasn't quite sure how CeeCee could stomach it. Unless I was mistaken, she felt the same way about him that he evidently felt about me. Only I didn't think his crush on me was very serious—if it had been, he wouldn't have been able to joke about it. CeeCee's crush on him, however, looked to me like the real thing. Oh, she was able to tease him and even insult him, but I'd looked into the rearview mirror a couple times and caught her looking at the back of his head in a manner that could only be called besotted.

But just when she was sure he wasn't looking.

When Adam pulled up in front of the Carmel hospital, I thought he had stopped at a country club or a private house by mistake. Okay, a really big private house, but hey, you should have seen some of the places in the Valley.

But then I saw a discreet little sign that said HOSPITAL. We piled out of the car and wandered through an immaculately kept garden, where the flower beds were bursting with blossoms. Hummingbirds buzzed all around, and I spotted some more of those palm trees I'd been sure I'd never see so far north of the equator.

At the information desk, I asked for Bryce Martinson's room. I wasn't sure he'd been admitted actually, but I knew from experience—unfortunately firsthand—that any accident in which a head wound might have occurred generally required an overnight stay for observation—and I was right. Bryce was there, and so was Father Dominic, conveniently situated right across the hall from one another.

We weren't the only people visiting these particular patients—not by a long shot. Bryce's room was packed. There wasn't, apparently, any limit on just how many people could crowd into a patient's room, and Bryce's looked as if it contained most of the Junipero Serra Mission Academy's senior class. In the middle of the sunny, cheerful room—where on every flat surface rested vases filled with flowers—lay Bryce in a shoulder cast, his right arm hanging from a pulley over his bed. He looked a lot better than he had that morning, mostly, I suppose, because he was pumped full of painkillers. When he saw me in the doorway, this big goofy smile broke out over his face, and he went, "Suze!"

Only he pronounced it "Soo-oo-ooze," so it sounded like it had more than one syllable.

"Uh, hi, Bryce," I said, suddenly shy. Everybody in the room had turned around to see who Bryce was talking to. Most of them were girls. They all did that thing a lot of girls do—they looked me over from the top of my head—I hadn't showered that morning because I'd been running so late, so I was not exactly having a good hair day—to the soles of my feet.

Then they smirked.

Not so Bryce would have noticed. But they did.

And even though I could not have cared less what a bunch of girls I had never met before, and would probably never meet again, thought of me, I blushed.

"Everybody," Bryce said. He sounded drunk, but pleasantly so. "This is Suze. Suze, this is everybody."

"Uh," I said. "Hi."

One of the girls, who was sitting on the end of Bryce's bed in a very white, wrinkle-free linen dress, went, "Oh, you're that girl who saved his life yesterday. Jake's new stepsister."

"Yeah," I said. "That's me." There was no way—no way—I was going to be able to ask Bryce what I needed to ask him with all these people in the room. CeeCee had steered Adam off into Father Dom's room in order to give me some time alone with Bryce, but it looked as if she'd done so in vain. There was no way I was going to get a minute with this guy alone. Not unless . . .

Well, not unless I asked for it.

"Hey," I said. "I need to talk to Bryce for a second. Do you guys mind?"

The girl on the end of the bed looked taken aback. "So talk to him. *We're* not stopping you."

I looked her right in the eye and said in my firmest mediation voice, "I need to talk to him *alone*."

Somebody whistled low and long. Nobody else moved. At least until Bryce went, "Hey, you guys. You heard her. Get out."

Thank God for morphine, that's all I have to say.

Grudgingly, the senior class filed out, everybody casting me dirty looks but Bryce, who lifted a hand connected to what looked like an IV and went, "Hey, Suze. C'mere and look at this."

I approached the bed. Now that we were the only people in it, I was able to see that Bryce actually had a very large room. It was also very cheerful, painted yellow, with a window that looked out over the garden outside.

"See what I got?" Bryce showed me a palm-sized instrument with a button on top of it. "My own painkiller pump. Anytime I feel pain, I just hit this button, and it releases codeine. Right into my bloodstream. Cool, huh?"

The guy was gone. That was obvious. Suddenly, I didn't think my mission was going to be so hard, after all.

"That's great, Bryce," I said. "I was real sorry to hear about your accident."

"Yeah." He giggled fatuously. "Too bad you weren't there. You might've been able to save me like you did yesterday."

"Yes," I said, clearing my throat uncomfortably. "You certainly do seem accident-prone these days."

"Yeah." His eyelids drifted closed, and for one panicky minute, I thought he'd gone to sleep. Then he opened his eyes and looked at me kind of sadly. "Suze, I don't think I'm going to be able to make it."

I stared at him. God, what a baby! "Of course you're going to make it. You've got a busted collarbone, is all. You'll be better in no time."

He giggled. "No, no. I mean, I don't think I'm going to be able to make it to our date on Saturday night."

"Oh," I said, blinking. "Oh, no, of course not. I didn't think so. Listen, Bryce, I need to ask you a favor. You're going to think it's weird"—actually, doped up as he was, I doubted he'd think it weird at all—"but I was wondering whether, back when you and Heather were going out, did she ever, um, give you anything?"

He blinked at me groggily. "Give me anything? You mean like a present?"

"Yes."

"Well, yeah. She got me a cashmere sweater vest for Christmas."

I nodded. A cashmere sweater vest wasn't going to do me any good. "Okay. Anything else? Maybe . . . a picture of herself?"

"Oh," he said. "Sure, sure. She gave me her school picture."

"She did?" I tried not to look too excited. "Any chance you've got it on you? In your wallet, maybe?" It was a gamble, I knew, but most people only clean out their wallets once a year or so. . . .

He screwed up his face. I guess thinking must have been painful for him since I saw him give himself a couple pumps of painkiller. Then his face relaxed. "Sure," he said. "I've still got her picture. My wallet's in that drawer there."

I opened the drawer to the table beside his bed. His wallet was indeed there, a slim black leather deal. I lifted it up and opened it. Heather's photo was jammed between a gold American Express card and a ski lift ticket. It showed her looking extremely glam, with all her long blonde hair flowing over one shoulder, staring coquettishly into the camera. In my school pictures, I always look like somebody just yelled, "Fire!" I couldn't believe this guy, who'd been dating a girl who looked like that, would bother asking a girl like me out.

"Can I borrow this picture?" I asked. "I just need it for a little while. I'll give it right back." This was a lie, but I didn't figure he'd give it to me otherwise.

"Sure, sure," he said, waving a hand.

"Thanks." I slipped the photo into my back-pack just as a tall woman in her forties came striding in wearing a lot of gold jewelry and carrying a box of pastries.

"Bryce, darling," she said. "Where did all your little friends go? I went all the way to the patisserie to get some snacks."

"Oh, they'll be back in a minute, Mom," Bryce said sleepily. "This is Suze. She saved my life yesterday."

Mrs. Martinson held out a smooth, tanned right hand. "Lovely to meet you, Susan," she said, giving my fingers the slightest of squeezes. "Can you believe what happened to poor little Bryce? His father's furious. As if things hadn't been going badly enough, what with that wretched girl—well, you know. And now this. I swear, it's like that academy was cursed, or something."

I said, "Yes. Well, nice to meet you. I'd better be going."

Nobody protested against my departure—Mrs. Martinson because she couldn't have cared less, and Bryce because he'd fallen asleep.

I found Adam and CeeCee standing outside a room across the hall. As I walked up to them, CeeCee put a finger to her lips. "Listen," she said.

I did as she asked.

"It simply couldn't have come at a worse time," a familiar voice—male, older—was saying. "What with the archbishop's visit not two weeks away—"

"I'm so sorry, Constantine." Father Dominic's voice sounded weak. "I know what a strain this must all be to you."

"And Bryce Martinson, of all people! Do you know who his father is? Only one of the best trial lawyers in Salinas!"

"Father Dom's getting reamed," Adam whispered to me. "Poor old guy."

"I wish he'd tell Monsignor Constantine to just go and jump in a lake." CeeCee's purple eyes flashed. "Dried-up, crusty old—"

I whispered, "Let's see if we can help him out. Maybe you guys could distract the monsignor. Then I'll just see if Father Dom needs anything. You know. Just real quick before we go."

CeeCee shrugged. "Fine with me."

"I'm game," Adam said.

So I called loudly, "Father Dominic?" and banged into the Father's hospital room.

The room wasn't as big as Bryce's or as cheerful. The walls were beige, not yellow, and there was only one vase with flowers in it. The window looked out, as near as I could tell, over the parking lot. And nobody had hooked Father Dominic up to any self-pumped painkiller machine. I don't know what kind of insurance priests have, but it was nowhere as good as it should have been.

To say that Father Dominic looked surprised to see me would have been an understatement. His mouth dropped open. He seemed perfectly incapable of saying anything. But that was okay because CeeCee came bustling in after me, and went, "Oh, Monsignor! Great. We've been looking all over for you. We'd like to do an exclusive, if that's okay, on how last night's act of vandalism is going to affect the upcoming visit of the archbishop. Adversely, right? Do you have any comments? Maybe you could step out here into the hallway where my associate and I can—"

Looking flustered, Monsignor Constantine followed CeeCee out the door with an irritated, "Now see here, young lady—"

I sauntered over to Father Dominic's side. I wasn't exactly excited to see him. I mean, I knew he probably wasn't too happy with me. I was the one whom Heather had thrown Father Serra's head at, and I figured he probably knew it and probably wasn't feeling too warmly toward me.

That's what I figured, anyway. But of course, I figured wrong. I'm pretty good at figuring out what dead people are thinking, but I haven't quite gotten the hang of the living yet.

"Susannah," Father Dominic said in his gentle voice. "What are you doing here? Is everything all right? I've been very concerned about you—"

I guess I should have expected it. Father Dominic wasn't sore at me at all. Just worried, that was all. But *he* was the one who needed worrying over. Aside from the nasty gash above one eye, his color was off. He looked gray, and much older than he actually was. Only his eyes, blue as the sky outside, looked like they always did, bright and filled with intelligent good humor.

Still, it made me mad all over again, seeing him like that. Heather didn't know it, but she was in for it, and how.

"Me?" I stared at him. "What are you worried about *me* for? *I'm* not the one who got clobbered by a crucifix this morning."

Father Dom smiled ruefully. "No, but I believe you do have a little explaining to do. Why didn't you tell me, Susannah? Why didn't you tell me what you had in mind? If I had known you planned on showing up at the Mission alone in the middle of the night, I never would have allowed it."

"Exactly why I didn't tell you," I said. "Look, Father, I'm sorry about the statue and Mr.

Walden's door and all that. But I had to try talking to her myself, don't you see? Woman to woman. I didn't know she was going to go postal on me."

"What did you expect? Susannah, you saw what she tried to do to that young man yesterday—"

"Yeah, but I could understand that. I mean, she loved him. She's really mad at him. I didn't think she'd try to go after *me*. I mean, *I* had nothing to do with it. I just tried to let her know her options—"

"Which is what I'd been doing ever since she first showed up at the Mission."

"Right. But Heather's not liking any of the options we've put before her. I'm telling you, the girl's gone loco. She's quiet now because she thinks she killed Bryce, and she's probably all tuckered out, but in a little while she's going to perk up again, and God only knows what she'll do next now that she knows what she's capable of."

Father Dominic looked at me curiously, his concern over the archbishop's impending visit forgotten. "What do you mean 'now that she knows what she's capable of'?"

"Well, last night was just a dress rehearsal. We can expect bigger and better things from Heather now that she knows what she can do."

Father Dominic shook his head, confused. "Have you seen her today? How do you know all this?"

I couldn't tell Father Dominic about Jesse. I really couldn't. It wasn't any of his business, for one thing. But I also had an idea it might kind of shock him, knowing there was this guy living in my bedroom. I mean, Father Dom was a priest and all.

"Look," I said. "I've been giving this a lot of thought, and I don't see any other way. You've tried to reason with her, and so have I. And look where it's gotten us. You're in the hospital, and I'm having to look over my shoulder everywhere I go. I think it's time to settle the matter once and for all."

Father Dom blinked at me. "What do you mean, Susannah? What are you talking about?"

I took a deep breath. "I'm talking about what we mediators do as a last resort."

He still looked confused. "Last resort? I'm afraid I don't know what you mean."

"I'm talking," I said, "about an exorcism."

# chapter sixteen

"Out of the question," said Father Dominic.

"Look," I said. "I don't see any other way. She won't go willingly, we both know that. And she's too dangerous to let hang around indefinitely. I think we're going to have to give her a push."

Father Dominic looked away from me, and started staring bleakly at a spot on the ceiling above our heads. "That isn't what we're here for, people like you and me, Susannah," he said in the saddest voice I had ever heard. "We are the sentries who guard the gates of the afterlife. We are the ones who help guide lost souls to their final destinations. And every single one of the spirits I've helped have passed my gate quite willingly. . . ."

Yeah. And if you clap hard enough, Tinkerbell won't die. It must, I thought, have been nice to see the world through Father Dom's eyes. It seemed like a nice place. A lot better than the world *I'd* lived in for the past sixteen years.

"Yes," I said. "Well, I don't see any other way."

"An exorcism," Father Dominic murmured. He said the word like it was distasteful, like mucus or something.

"Look," I said, beginning to regret I'd said anything. "Believe me, it's not a method I recommend. But I don't see that we have much choice. Heather's not just a danger to Bryce anymore." I didn't want to tell him what she'd said about David. I could just see him jumping out of bed and hollering for a pair of crutches. But since I had already let spill what I was planning, I had to let him know why I felt such an extreme was necessary. "She's a danger to the whole school," I said. "She's got to be stopped."

He nodded. "Yes. Yes, of course, you're right. But Susannah, you've got to promise me you won't try it until I've been released. I was talking to the doctor, and she says she might let me go as early as Friday. That will give us plenty of time to research the proper methodology—" He glanced at his bedside table. "Hand me that Bible there, would you, Susannah? If we can get the wording correctly, we just might—"

I handed him the Bible. "I'm pretty sure," I said, "that I've got it down pat."

He lifted his gaze, pinning me with those baby blues of his. Too bad he was so old, and a priest, besides. I wondered how many hearts he'd broken back before he'd gotten his calling. "How could you possibly," he wondered, "have gotten anything as complicated as a Roman Catholic exorcism down pat?"

I fidgeted uncomfortably. "Well, I wasn't really planning on doing the Roman Catholic version."

"Is there another?"

"Oh, sure. Most religions have one. Personally, I prefer Mecumba. It's pretty much to the point. No long incantations or anything."

He looked pained. "Mecumba?"

"Sure. Brazilian voodoo. I got if off the Net. All you need is some chicken blood and a—"

"Mary, mother of God," Father Dominic interrupted. Then, when he'd recovered himself, he said, "Out of the question. Heather Chambers was baptized a Roman Catholic, and despite the cause of her death, she deserves a Roman Catholic exorcism, if not burial. Her chances of being admitted into heaven at this point aren't great, I'll admit, but I certainly intend to see that she gets every opportunity to greet St. Peter at the gates."

"Father Dom," I said. "I really don't think it matters whether she gets a Roman Catholic exorcism or a Brazilian one, or a Pygmy one, for that matter. The fact is, if there is a heaven, there's no way Heather Chambers is getting in there."

Father Dominic made a *tut-tutt*ing noise. "Susannah, how can you say such a thing? There is good in everyone. Surely even you can see that."

"Even me? What do you mean, even me?"

"Well, I mean even Susannah Simon, who can be very hard on others, must see that even in the cruelest human being there can exist a flower of good. Maybe just the tiniest blossom, in need of water and sunlight, but a flower just the same."

I wondered what kind of painkillers Father Dom was on.

I said, "Well, okay, Father. All I know is, wherever Heather's going, it ain't heaven. If there *is* a heaven."

He smiled at me sadly. "I wish," he said, "you had half as much faith in the good Lord, Susannah, as you have courage. Listen to me now for a moment. You mustn't—you *must not*—

attempt to stop Heather on your own. It is extremely clear that she very nearly killed you last night. I could not believe my eyes when I walked out and saw the damage she caused. You were lucky to escape with your life. And it is clear from what happened this morning that, like you say, she is only growing stronger. It would be stupid—criminally stupid—of you to try to do anything on your own again."

I knew he was right. What's more, if I really did go through with the exorcism thing, I couldn't let Jesse help me . . . the exorcism might send him back to his maker, right along with Heather.

"Besides," Father Dominic said. "There isn't any reason to hurry, is there? Now that she's managed to hospitalize Bryce, she won't be up to any more mischief—at least not until he comes back to school. He seems to be the only person she entertains murderous feelings toward—"

I didn't say anything. How could I? I mean, the poor guy looked so pathetic lying there. I didn't want to give him more to worry about. But the truth was, I couldn't possibly wait for Father Dom to get out of the hospital. Heather meant business. With every day that passed, she would only get stronger and nastier, and more filled with hate. I had to get rid of her, and I had to get rid of her soon.

So I committed what I'm sure must be some kind of mortal sin. I lied to a priest.

Good thing I'm not Catholic.

"Don't worry, Father Dom," I said. "I'll wait till you're feeling better."

Father Dominic was no dummy, though. He went, "Promise me, Susannah."

I said, "I promise."

I had my fingers crossed, of course. I hoped that, if there was a God, this would cancel out the sin of lying to one of his most deserving servants.

"Let me see," Father Dominic was murmuring. "We'll need holy water, of course. That's no problem. And, of course, a crucifix."

As he was muttering over his exorcism grocery list, Adam and CeeCee came into the room.

"Hey, Father Dom," Adam said. "Boy, do you look terrible."

CeeCee elbowed him. *"Adam,"* she hissed. Then, to the Father, she said brightly, "Don't listen to him, Father Dom. I think you look great. Well, for a guy with a bunch of broken bones, I mean."

"Children." Father Dominic looked really happy to see them. "What a delight! But why are you wasting a beautiful afternoon like this one visiting an old man in a hospital? You ought to be down at the beach enjoying the nice weather."

"We're actually here doing an article for the *Mission News* about the accident," CeeCee said. "We just got done interviewing the monsignor. It's really unfortunate, about the archbishop coming, and all, and the statue of Father Serra not having a head."

"Yeah," Adam said. "A real bummer."

"Well," Father Dominic said. "Never mind that. It's the caring spirit of you children that should most impress the archbishop."

"Amen," said Adam solemnly.

Before either of us had a chance to berate Adam for being sarcastic, a nurse came in and told CeeCee and me that we had to leave because she had to give Father Dom his sponge bath.

"Sponge bath," Adam grumbled as we made our way back to the car. "Father Dom gets a sponge bath, but me, a guy who can actually appreciate something like that, what do *I* get?"

"A chance to play chauffeur to the two most beautiful girls in Carmel?" CeeCee offered helpfully.

"Yeah," Adam said. "Right." Then he glanced

at me. "Not that you aren't the most beautiful girl in Carmel, Suze. . . . I just meant . . . Well, *you* know. . . ."

"I know," I said with a smile.

"I mean, a sponge bath. And did you get a look at that nurse?" Adam held the passenger seat forward so CeeCee could crawl into the backseat. "There must be something to this priest thing. Maybe I should enroll."

From the backseat CeeCee said, "You don't enroll, you receive a calling. And believe me, Adam, you wouldn't like it. They don't let priests play Nintendo."

Adam digested this. "Maybe I could form a new order," he said, thoughtfully. "Like the Franciscans, only we'd be the Joystick Order. Our motto would be High Score for One, Pizza for All."

CeeCee said, "Look out for that seagull."

We were on Carmel Beach Road. Just beyond the low stone wall to our right was the Pacific, lit up like a jewel by the enormous yellow ball of sun hovering above it. I guess I must have been looking at it a little longingly—I still hadn't gotten used to seeing it all the time—because Adam went, "Aw, hell," and zipped into a parking space that a BMW had just vacated. I looked at him questioningly as he threw the car into park, and he said, "What? You don't have time to sit and watch the sunset?"

I was out of the car in a flash.

How, I wondered a little while later, had I ever not looked forward to moving here? Sitting on a blanket Adam had extricated from the trunk of his car, watching the joggers and the evening surfers, the Frisbee-catching dogs and the tourists with their cameras, I felt better than I had in a long time. It might have been the fact that I was still operating on about four hours of sleep. It might have been that the heavy odor of brine was clouding my senses. But I really felt, for the first time in what seemed like forever, at peace.

Which was weird, considering the fact that in a few hours, I was going to be doing battle with the forces of evil.

But until then, I decided to enjoy myself. I turned my face toward the setting sun, feeling its warming rays on my cheeks, and listened to the roaring of the waves, the shrieking of the gulls, and the chatter of CeeCee and Adam.

"So I said to her, 'Claire, you're nearly forty. If you and Paul want to have another kid, you had better hurry. Time is not on your side.'" Adam sipped a latte he'd picked up from a coffee shop near where we'd parked. "And she was all, 'But your father and I don't want you to feel threatened by the new baby,' and I was like, 'Claire, babies don't threaten me.' You know what makes me feel threatened? Steroid-popping Neanderthals like Brad Ackerman. *They* threaten me."

CeeCee shot Adam a warning look, then looked at me. "How are you getting along with your new stepbrothers, Suze?"

I tore my eyes away from the setting sun. "All right, I guess. Does Do—I mean, Brad really take steroids?"

Adam said, "I shouldn't have mentioned that. I'm sorry. I'm sure he doesn't. All those guys on the wrestling team, though—they scare me. And they're so homophobic . . . well, you can't help wondering about their sexual orientation. I mean, they all think *I'm* gay, but you wouldn't catch *me* in a pair of tights grabbing at some other guy's inner thigh."

I felt a need to apologize for my stepbrother, and did so, adding, "I'm not so sure he's gay. He got very excited when Kelly Prescott called the other night and invited us to her pool party on Saturday."

Adam whistled, and CeeCee said unexpectedly,

"Well, well, well. Are you sure this blanket is good enough for you? Maybe you would prefer a cashmere beach blanket. That's what Kelly and all her friends sit on."

I blinked at them, realizing I'd just committed a *faux pas*. "Oh, I'm sorry. Kelly didn't invite you guys? But I just assumed she was inviting all the sophomores."

"Certainly not," CeeCee said with a sniff. "Just the sophomores with status, which Adam and I definitely lack."

"But you," I said, "are the editor of the school paper."

"Right," Adam said. "Translate that into *dork*, and you'll have an idea why we've never been invited to any of Princess Kelly's pool parties."

"Oh," I said. I was quiet for a minute, listening to the waves. Then I said, "Well, it's not like I was planning on going."

"You weren't?" CeeCee's eyes bugged out behind her glasses.

"No. At first because I had a date with Bryce, which is off now. But now because . . . well, if you guys aren't going, who would I talk to?"

CeeCee leaned back on the blanket. "Suze," she said. "Have you ever considered running for class VP?"

I laughed. "Oh, right. I'm the new kid, remember?"

"Yeah," Adam said. "But there's something about you. I saw real leadership potential in the way you trounced Debbie Mancuso yesterday. Guys always admire girls who look as if any minute they might punch another girl in the mouth. We just can't help it." He shrugged. "Maybe it's in the genes."

"Well," I said with a laugh. "I'll certainly take it under advisement. I did hear a rumor Kelly was planning on blowing the entire class budget on some kind of dance—"

"Right." CeeCee nodded. "She does that every year. The stupid spring dance. It's so boring. I mean, if you don't have a boyfriend, what is the point? There's nothing to do there but dance."

"Wait," Adam said. "Remember that time we brought the water balloons?"

"Well," CeeCee amended. "Okay, *that* year was fun."

"I was kind of thinking," I heard myself saying, "that something like this might be better. You know. A cookout at the beach. Maybe a couple of them."

"Hey," Adam said. "Yeah! And a bonfire! The pyro in me has always wanted to do a bonfire on the beach."

CeeCee said, "Totally. That's totally what we should do. Suze, you've *got* to run for VP."

Holy smoke, what had I done? I didn't want to be sophomore class VP! I didn't want to get involved! I had no school spirit—I had no opinion on anything! What was I doing? Had I lost my mind?

"Oh, look," Adam said, pointing suddenly at the sun. "There it goes."

The great orange ball seemed to sink into the sea as it began its slow descent below the horizon. I didn't see any splashing or steam, but I could have sworn I heard it hit the water's surface.

"There goes the sun," CeeCee sang softly.

"Da da da da," Adam said.

"There goes the sun," I joined in.

Okay, I have to admit, it was kind of childish, sitting there singing, watching the sun go down. But it was also kind of fun. Back in New York, we used to sit in the park and watch the undercover cops arrest drug dealers. But that wasn't anywhere near as nice as this, singing happily on a beach as the sun went down.

Something strange was happening. I wasn't sure what it was.

"And I say," the three of us sang, "it's all right!"

And, strangely enough, at that moment, I actually believed it would be. All right, I mean.

And that's when I realized what was happening: I was fitting in. Me, Susannah Simon, mediator. I was fitting in somewhere for the first time in my life.

And I was happy about it. Really happy. I actually believed, just then, that everything was going to be all right.

Boy, was I ever in denial.

# chapter seventeen

My alarm went off at midnight. I didn't hit the snooze button. I turned it off, clapped my hands to turn on the bedside lamp, rolled over, and stared at the canopy over my bed.

This was it. D-day. Or E-day, I should have called it.

I'd been so tired after dinner, I knew I'd never make it without a nap. I told my mother I was going upstairs to do homework, and then I'd lain down with the intention of sacking out for a few hours. Back in our old place in Brooklyn, this wouldn't have been a problem. My mom would have left me alone like I asked. But in the Ackerman household, the words *I want to be alone* were apparently completely meaningless. And not because the place is crawling with ghosts, either. No, it was the living who kept on bugging me for a change.

First it was Dopey. When I'd sat down to another gourmet dinner, immaculately prepared by my new stepfather, an interrogation of sorts had begun because I had ended up not getting home until after 6:00. There was the usual "Where were you?" from my mother (even though I'd so conscientiously left her that explanatory message). Then a "Did you have fun?" from Andy. And then there was a "Who'd you go with?" from, of all people, Doc. And when I said, "Adam McTavish and CeeCee Webb," Dopey actually snorted disgustedly and, chewing on a meatball, said, "Christ. The class freaks."

Andy said, "Hey. Watch it."

"Well, jeez, Dad," Dopey said. "One's a freakin' albino and the other's a fag."

This earned him a very hard wallop on the head from his father, who also grounded him for a week. Meaning, I couldn't help pointing out to Dopey later as we were clearing our plates from the table, that he would be unable to attend Kelly Prescott's pool party, which, by the way, I—Queen of the Freaks—had gotten him invited to.

"Too bad, bubby," I said, giving Dopey a sympathetic pat on the cheek.

He slapped my hand away. "Yeah?" he said. "Well, at least nobody'll be callin' *me* a fag hag tomorrow."

"Oh, sweetie," I said. I reached out and tweaked the cheek I'd just patted. "You'll never have to worry about people calling you that. They call you *much* worse things."

He hit my hand again, his fury apparently so great, it rendered him temporarily speechless.

"Promise me you'll never change," I begged him. "You're so adorable just the way you are."

Dopey called me a very bad name just as his father entered the kitchen with the remains of the salad.

Andy grounded him for another week, and then sent him to his room. To show his unhappiness with this turn of events, Dopey put on the Beastie Boys and played them at such high decibels that sleep was impossible for me . . . at least until Andy came up and took away Dopey's speakers. Then everything got very quiet, and I was just about to doze off when someone tapped at my door. It was Doc.

"Um," he said, glancing nervously past me, into the darkness of my room—the "haunted" room of the house. "Is this a good time to, um, talk about the things I found out? About the house, I mean? And the people who died here?"

"People? In the plural sense?"

"Oh, sure," Doc said. "I was able to find a surprising amount of documentation listing the crimes committed in this house, many of which involved murder of varying degrees. Because it was a boardinghouse, there were any number of transient residents, most of whom were on their way home after striking it rich in the Gold Rush farther upstate. Many of them were killed in their sleep and their gold absconded with, some thought by the owners of the establishment, but most likely it was by other residents—"

Fearing I was going to hear that Jesse had died this way—and suddenly not at all eager to know anymore what had caused his death, particularly not if he happened to be around to overhear—I said, "Listen, Doc—I mean, Dave. I don't think I've gotten over my jet lag yet, so I'm trying to catch up a little on my sleep just now. Can we talk about this tomorrow at school? Maybe we could have lunch together."

Doc's eyes widened. "Are you serious? You want to have lunch with me?"

I stared at him. "Well, yeah. Why? Is there

some rule high schoolers can't eat with middle schoolers?"

"No," Doc said. "It's just that . . . they never do."

"Well," I said. "I will. Okay? You buy the drinks, and I'll buy dessert."

"Great!" Doc said, and went back to his own room looking like I'd just said tomorrow I'd present him with the throne of England.

I was just on the verge of dozing off again when there was another knock on the door. This time when I opened it, Sleepy was standing there looking more wide awake, for once, than I felt.

"Look," he said. "I don't care if you're gonna take the car out at night, just put the keys back on the hook, okay?"

I stared up at him. "I haven't been taking your car out at night, Slee—I mean, Jake."

He said, "Whatever. Just put the keys back where you found 'em. And it wouldn't hurt if you pitched in for gas now and then."

I said slowly, so he would understand, "I haven't been taking your car out at night, Jake."

"What you do on your own time is your business," Sleepy said. "I mean, I don't think gangs are cool or anything. But it's your life. Just put my keys back so I can find 'em."

I could see there was no point in arguing this,

so I said, "Okay, I will," and shut the door.

After that, I got a good few hours of much needed sleep. I didn't exactly wake up feeling refreshed—I could have slept for maybe another year—but I felt a little better, at least.

Good enough to go kick some ghost butt, anyway.

Earlier in the evening, I'd gotten together all the things I was going to need. My backpack was crammed with candles, paintbrushes, a Tupperware container of chicken blood that I'd bought at the butcher counter in the Safeway I made Adam take me to before dropping me off at home, and various other assorted necessary components of a real Brazilian exorcism. I was completely ready to go. All I had to do was throw on my high tops, and I was out of there.

Except, of course, Jesse had to show up just as I was jumping off the porch roof.

"Okay," I said, straightening up, my feet smarting a little in spite of the soft ground I'd landed on. "Let's get one thing straight right now. You are not going to show up down at the Mission tonight. Got that? You show up down there, and you are going to be very, very sorry."

Jesse was leaning against one of the giant pine trees in our yard. Just leaning there, his arms folded across his chest, looking at me as if I were some sort of interesting sideshow attraction or something.

"I mean it," I said. "It's going to be a bad night for ghosts. Real bad. So I wouldn't show up down there if I were you."

Jesse, I noticed, was smiling. There wasn't as much moon as there'd been the night before, but there was enough so that I could see that the little curl at the corners of his lips was turning skyward, not down.

"Susannah," he said. "What are you up to?"

"Nothing." I marched over to the carport, and yanked out the ten-speed. "I just got some things to settle."

Jesse strolled over toward me as I was strapping on the bike helmet. "With Heather?" he asked lightly.

"Right. With Heather. I know things got out of hand last time, but this time, things are going to be different."

"How, precisely?"

I swung a leg over that stupid bar they put on boys' bikes, and stood at the top of the driveway, my fingers curled around the handlebars. "Okay," I said. "I'll level with you. I'm going to perform an exorcism."

His right hand shot out. It gripped the bar between my fingers. "A *what*?" he said in a voice completely devoid of the good humor that had been in it before.

I swallowed. Okay, I wasn't feeling quite as confident as I was acting. In fact, I was practically quaking in my Converse All Stars. But what else could I do? I had to stop Heather before she hurt anybody else. And it would have been really helpful if everybody could have just supported me in my efforts.

"You can't help me," I said woodenly. "You can't go down there tonight, Jesse, or you might get exorcized, too."

"You," Jesse said, speaking as tonelessly as I was, "are insane."

"Probably," I said miserably.

"She'll kill you," Jesse said. "Don't you understand? That's what she wants."

"No." I shook my head. "She doesn't want to kill me. She wants to kill everybody I care about first. *Then* she wants to kill me." I sniffled. For some reason, my nose was running. Probably because it was so cold out. I don't see how those palm trees could stay alive. It was like forty degrees or something, outside.

"But I'm not going to let her, see?" I continued.

"I'm going to stop her. Now let go of my bike."

Jesse shook his head. "No. No. Even you wouldn't do something so stupid."

"Even me?" I was hurt, in spite of myself. "Thanks."

He ignored me. "Does the priest know about this, Susannah? Did you tell the priest?"

"Um, sure. He knows. He's, uh, meeting me there."

"The priest is meeting you there?"

"Yeah, uh-huh." I gave a shaky laugh. "You don't think I'd try something like this on my own, do you? I mean, jeez, I'm not *that* stupid, no matter what you might think."

His grip on the bike relaxed a little. "Well, if the priest will be there . . ."

"Sure. Sure he will."

The grip tightened again. Jesse's other hand came around, and a long finger wagged in my face as he said, "You're lying, aren't you? The priest isn't going to be there at all. She hurt him, didn't she? This morning? I thought so. Did she kill him?"

I shook my head. I didn't feel so much like talking all of a sudden. It felt like there was something in my throat. Something that hurt.

"That's why you're so angry," Jesse said wonderingly. "I should have known. You're going down there to get even with her for what she did to the priest."

"So what if I am?" I exploded. "She deserves it!"

He put his finger down, gripping the handlebars of my bike with both hands. And let me tell you, he was pretty strong for a dead guy. I couldn't budge the stupid thing with him hanging on to it like that.

"Susannah," he said. "This isn't the way. This wasn't why you were given this extraordinary gift, not so you could do things like—"

"Gift!" I nearly burst out laughing. I had to grit my teeth to keep from doing so. "Yeah, that's right, Jesse. I've been given a precious gift. Well, you know what? I'm sick of it. I really am. I thought coming out here, I'd be able to make a new start. I thought things might be different. And you know what? They are. They're *worse*."

"Susannah—"

"What am I supposed to do, Jesse? Love Heather for what she did? Embrace her wounded spirit? I'm sorry, but that's impossible. Maybe Father Dom could do it, but not me, and he's out of commission, so we're going to do things *my* way. I'm going to get rid of her, and if you know what's good for you, Jesse, you'll stay away!"

I gave my kickstand a vicious kick, and at the same time, yanked on the handlebars. The move surprised Jesse so much, he let go of the bike involuntarily. A second later, I was off, spraying gravel out from beneath my back wheel, leaving Jesse in my dust. I heard him say a bunch of stuff in Spanish as I sped down the driveway. I think it was probably swear words. The word *querida* was definitely not mentioned.

I didn't see much of my trip down into the valley. The wind was so cold that tears streamed in a pretty constant flow down my cheeks and back into my hair. There wasn't much traffic out, thank God, so when I flew through the intersection, it didn't really matter that I couldn't see. The cars stopped for me, anyway.

I knew it was going to be trickier to break into the school this time. They'd have beefed up the security in response to what had happened the night before. Beefed up the security? All they had to do was actually get some.

And they had. A police cruiser sat in the parking lot, its lights off. Just sitting there, the moonlight reflecting off the closed windows. The driver—doubtlessly some luckless rookie to have pulled so boring an assignment—was probably listening to music, though I couldn't hear any from where I stood just outside the gate to the parking lot.

So I was going to have to find another way to get in. No biggie. I stashed the bike in some bushes, then took a leisurely stroll around the perimeter of the school.

There aren't many buildings you can keep a fairly slender sixteen-year-old girl out of. I mean, we're pretty flexible. I happen to be double-jointed in a lot of places, too. I won't tell you how I managed to break in, since I don't want the school authorities figuring it out—you never know, I might have to do it again someday—but let's just say if you're going to make a gate, make sure it reaches all the way to the ground. That gap between the cement and where the gate starts is exactly all the room a girl like me needs to wriggle through.

Inside the courtyard, things looked a lot different than they had the night before—and a whole lot creepier. All the floodlights were turned off—this didn't seem like a very good safety precaution to me, but it was possible, of course, that Heather had blown all the bulbs—so the courtyard was dark and eerily shadowed. The fountain was turned off. I couldn't hear anything this time except for crickets. Just crickets chirping in the hibiscus. Nothing wrong with crickets. Crickets are our friends.

There was no sign of Heather. There was no sign of anybody. This was good.

I crept as quietly as I could—which was pretty quietly in my sneakers—to the locker Heather and I shared. Then I knelt down on the cold flagstones and opened my backpack.

I lit the candles first. I needed their light to see by. Holding my lighter—okay, it wasn't really my lighter, it was the long-handled lighter from the barbecue—to the candle's bottom, I dripped some wax onto the ground, then shoved the candle's base into the gooey drippings to keep it in place. I did this to each candle until I'd formed a ring of them in front of me. Then I peeled back the lid of the container holding the chicken blood.

I'm not going to write down the shape that I was required to paint in the center of the ring of candles in order for the exorcism to work. Exorcisms aren't things people should try at home, I don't care how badly you might be haunted. And they should only be performed by a professional like myself. You wouldn't, after all, want to hurt any innocent ghosts who happen to be hanging around. I mean, exorcizing

Grandma—that won't make you *too* unpopular, or anything.

And Mecumba—Brazilian voodoo—isn't something people should mess with, either, so I won't write down the incantation I had to say. It was all in Portuguese, anyway. But let's just say that I dipped my brush into the chicken blood and made the appropriate shapes, uttering the appropriate words as I did so. It wasn't until I reached into the backpack and pulled out Heather's photograph that I noticed the crickets had stopped chirping.

"What," she said in an irritated voice from just behind my right shoulder, "in the hell do you think you're doing?"

I didn't answer her. I put the photo in the center of the shape I had painted. The light from the candles illuminated it fairly well.

Heather came closer. "Hey," she said. "That's a picture of me. Where'd you get it?"

I didn't say anything except the Portuguese words I was supposed to say. This seemed to upset Heather.

Well, let's face it. Everything seemed to upset Heather.

"What are you doing?" Heather demanded again. "What's that language you're talking in?

And what's that red paint for?" When I didn't answer her, Heather became—as seemed to be her nature—abusive. "Hey, bitch," she said, laying a hand upon my shoulder and pulling on it, not very gently. "Are you listening to me?"

I broke off the incantation. "Could you do me a favor, Heather," I said, "and stand right there next to your picture?"

Heather shook her head. Her long blonde hair shimmered in the candlelight. "What are you?" she demanded rudely. "High or something? I'm not standing anywhere. Is that . . . is that blood?"

I shrugged. Her hand was still on my shoulder. "Yes," I said. "Don't worry, though. It's just chicken blood."

"Chicken blood?" Heather made a face. "Gross. Are you kidding me? What's it for?"

"To help you," I said. "To help you go back."

Heather's jaw tightened. The doors to the lockers in front of me began to rattle. Not a lot. Just enough to let me know Heather was unhappy. "I thought," she said, "that I made it pretty clear to you last night that I'm not going anywhere."

"You said you wanted to go back."

"Yeah," Heather said. The dials on the combination locks began to spin noisily. "To my old life."

"Well," I said. "I found a way you can do it."

The doors began to hum, they were shaking so hard.

"No way," Heather said.

"Way. All you have to do is stand right here, between those candles, next to your picture."

Heather needed no further urging. In a second, she was exactly where I wanted her.

"Are you sure this will work?" Heather asked excitedly.

"It better," I said. "Otherwise, I've blown my allowance on candles and chicken blood for nothing."

"And things will be just like they were? Before I died, I mean?"

"Sure," I said. Should I have felt guilty for lying to her? I didn't. Feel guilty, I mean. All I felt was relieved. It had all been too easy. "Now shut up a minute while I say the words."

She was only too eager to oblige. I said the words.

And said the words.

And said the words.

I was just starting to be worried nothing was going to happen when the candle flames flickered. And it wasn't because there was any wind.

"Nothing's happening," Heather complained,

but I shushed her.

The candle flames flickered again. And then, above Heather's head, where the roof of the breezeway should have been, appeared a hole filled with red, swirling gases. I stared at the hole.

"Uh, Heather," I said. "You might want to close your eyes."

She did so happily enough. "Why? Is it working?"

"Oh," I said. "It's working, all right."

Heather said something that might have been "goodie," but I wasn't sure. I couldn't hear her too well since the swirling red gas—it was more like smoke really—had started spiraling down from the hole, making a low sort of thundering noise as it did so. Soon long tendrils of the stuff were wrapping around Heather, lightly as fog. Only she didn't know it since her eyes were closed.

"I hear something," she said. "Is this it?"

Above her head, the hole had widened. I could see lightning flashing in it. It didn't look like the most pleasant place to go. I'm not saying I'd opened a gate to hell or anything—at least, I hope not—but it was definitely a dimension other than our own, and frankly, it didn't look like a nice place to visit, let alone live in for all eternity.

"Just one more minute," I said, as more and more snaky red limbs wrapped around her slender cheerleader's body. "And you'll be there."

Heather tossed her long hair. "Oh, God," she said. "I can't wait. First thing I'm going to do, I'm going to go down to the hospital and apologize to Bryce. Don't you think that's a good idea, Susie?"

I said, "Sure." The thunder was getting louder, the lightning more frequent. "That's a great idea."

"I hope my mom hasn't gotten rid of my clothes," Heather said. "Just because I was dead. You don't think my mom would have gotten rid of my clothes, do you, Susie?" She opened her eyes. "Do you?"

I shouted, "Keep your eyes closed!"

But it was too late. She had seen. Oh, boy, had she seen. She took one look at the red wisps wrapped around her and started shrieking.

And not with fear, either. Oh, no. Heather wasn't scared. She was mad. Really mad.

"You bitch!" she shrieked. "You aren't sending me back! You aren't sending me back at all! You're sending me *away*!"

And then, just when the thunder was getting loudest, Heather stepped out of the circle.

Just like that. She just stepped out of it. Like it was no big deal. Like it was a hopscotch square.

Those red wisps of smoke that had been wrapped all around her just fell away. Fell away like nothing. And the hole above Heather's head closed up.

Okay. I admit it. I got mad. Hey, I'd put a lot of work into this thing.

"Oh, no you don't," I growled. I strode up to Heather and grabbed her. Around the neck, I'm afraid.

"Get back in there," I said, from between gritted teeth. "Get back in there right now."

Heather only laughed. I had the girl by the throat, and she only laughed.

Behind her, though, the locker doors started humming again. More loudly than ever.

"You," she said, "are so dead. You are so dead, Simon. And you know what? I'm going to make sure that the rest of them go with you. All of your little freaky friends. And that stepbrother of yours, too."

I tightened my grip on her throat. "I don't think so. I think you're going to get back where you were and go away like a good little ghost."

She laughed again. "Make me," she said, her blue eyes glittering like crazy.

Well. If you put it that way.

I hit her hard with my right fist. Then, before she had a chance to recover, I hit her the other way with my left. If she felt the blows, she made no sign. No, that's not true. I know she felt the blows because the locker doors suddenly started opening and closing. Not closing, exactly. Slamming. Hard. Hard enough to shake the whole breezeway.

I mean it. The whole breezeway was pitching back and forth, as if the ground beneath it was really ocean waves. The thick wooden support pillars that held up the arched roof shook in ground that had held them steady for close to three hundred years. Three hundred years of earthquakes, fires, and floods, and the ghost of a cheerleader sends them tumbling down.

I tell you, this mediation stuff is no damned fun.

And then *her* fingers were around *my* throat. I don't know how. I guess I got distracted by all the shaking. This was no good. I grabbed her by the arms, and started trying to push her back toward the circle of candles. As I did so, I muttered the Portuguese incantation under my breath, staring at the swaying rafters overhead, hoping that the hole to that shadowy land would open up again.

"Shut up," Heather said, when she heard what I was saying. "Shut your mouth! You are not sending me away. I belong here! A lot more than you!"

I kept saying the words. I kept pushing.

"Who the hell do you think you are?" Heather's face was red with rage. Out of the corner of my eye, I saw a planter packed with geraniums levitate a few inches off the stone balustrade on which it had been resting. "You're *no one.* You've only been at this school two days. Two days! You think you can just come in here and change everything? You think you can just *take my place*? Who do you think you are?"

I kicked out a leg and, pulling on the arms I held at the same time as I swept her feet out from under her, sent us both crashing to the hard stone floor. The planter followed, not because we'd knocked it over, but because Heather sent it hurling through the air at me. I ducked at the last minute, and the heavy clay pot smashed against the locker doors in an explosion of mulch and geranium and pottery shards. I grabbed fistfuls of Heather's long, glossy, blonde hair. This was not very sporting of me, but hey, throwing the geraniums hadn't been very sporting of her.

She shrieked, kicking and writhing like an eel while I half dragged, half shoved her toward the circle of candles. She'd started levitating other objects. The combination locks spun out of their cores in the locker doors, and careened through the air at me like tiny little flying saucers. Then a tornado rolled in, sucking the contents of those lockers out into the breezeway, so that textbooks and three-ring binders were flying at me from four directions. I kept my head down, but didn't lose my hold on her even when somebody's trig book hit me hard in the shoulder. I kept saying the words I knew would open the hole again.

"Why are you doing this?" Heather shrieked. "Why can't you just leave me alone?"

"Because." I was bruised, I was out of breath, I was dripping with sweat, and all I wanted to do was let go of her, turn around and go home, crawl into my bed, and sleep for a million years.

But I couldn't.

So instead, I kicked her in the center of the chest and sent her staggering back to the center of the circle of candles. And the minute she stumbled over that photograph of herself she'd given to Bryce, the hole that had opened up above her head reappeared. And this time, the red smoke closed around her as suffocatingly as a thick wool blanket. She wasn't breaking out again. Not that easily.

The red fog had encased her so thickly, I couldn't see her anymore, but I could sure hear her. Her shrieks ought to have waked the dead—

except, of course, she was the only dead around. Thunder clapped over her head. Inside the black hole that had opened above her, I thought I saw stars twinkling.

"*Why?*" Heather screamed. "Why are you doing this to me?"

"Because," I said. "I'm the mediator."

And then two things happened almost simultaneously.

The red smoke surrounding Heather began to be sucked back up into the spinning hole, taking Heather with it.

And the sturdy pillars that supported the breezeway over my head suddenly snapped in two as cleanly as if they'd been two inches, and not two feet, thick.

And then the breezeway collapsed on top of me.

# chapter eighteen

I have no idea how long I lay beneath the planks of wood and heavy clay tiles of the crumpled breezeway. Looking back, I realize I must have lost consciousness, if only for a few minutes.

All I can remember is something sharp hitting me on the head, and the next thing I knew, I'd opened my eyes to consummate blackness, and a feeling that I was being smothered.

A favorite trick of some poltergeists is to sit on their victim's chest while he or she is just waking, so that the poor soul feels he or she is being smothered, but can't see why. I couldn't see why, and for a second or two I thought I'd failed and that Heather was still in this world, sitting on my chest, torturing me, getting her revenge for what I'd tried to do.

Then I thought, *Maybe I'm dead.*

I don't know why. But it occurred to me. Maybe this was how being dead felt. At first, anyway. This must have been how it was for Heather when she woke up in her coffin. She must have felt the same way I did: trapped, suffocated, frightened witless. God, no wonder she'd been in such a bad mood all the time. No wonder she'd wanted so desperately to get back to the world she'd known pre-death. This was horrible. It was worse than horrible. It was hell.

But then I moved my hand—the only part of me I *could* move—and felt something rough and cool resting over me. That's when I knew what had happened. The breezeway had collapsed. Heather had used her last little bit of kinetic power to hurt me for sending her away. And she'd done a splendid job because here I was unable to move, trapped underneath who knew how many pounds of wood and Spanish tile.

Thanks, Heather. Thanks a lot.

I should have been scared. I mean, there I was pinned down, completely unable to move, in utter darkness. But before I had time to start panicking, I heard someone call my name. I thought at first I might be going crazy. Nobody knew, after all, that I'd gone down to the school except for Jesse, of course, and I'd told him what would happen if he showed up. He wasn't stupid. He knew I was performing an exorcism. Could he have decided to come down, anyway? Was it safe yet? I didn't know. If he happened to step into the circle of candles and chicken blood, would he be sucked into that same dark shadowland that took Heather?

Now I started to panic.

"Jesse!" I yelled, pounding on the wood above my head, causing dirt and bits of wood to fall down onto my face. "Don't!" I shrieked. All the dust was making me choke, but I didn't care. "Go back! It isn't safe!"

Then a great weight was lifted off my chest, and suddenly I could see. Above me stretched the night sky, velvet blue and spotted with a dusting of stars. And framed by those stars hung a face hovering over me worriedly.

"Here she is," Doc called, his voice wobbling in both pitch and volume. "Jake, I found her!"

A second face joined the first one, this one framed by a curtain of over-long blond hair. "Jesus Christ," Sleepy drawled, when he got a look at me. "Are you all right, Suze?"

I nodded dazedly. "Help me up," I said.

The two of them managed to get most of the bigger pieces of timber off me. Then Sleepy instructed me to wrap my arms around his neck, which I did, while David grabbed my waist. And with the two of them pulling, and me pushing with my feet, I finally managed to get clear of the rubble.

We sat for a minute in the darkness of the courtyard, leaning against the edge of the dais on which the headless statue of Junipero Serra stood. We just sat there, panting and staring at the ruin which had once been our school. Well, that's a bit dramatic, I guess. Most of the school was still standing. Even most of the breezeway was still up. Just the section in front of Heather's locker and Mr. Walden's classroom had come down. The twisted pile of wood neatly hid the evidence of my evening's activities, including the candles, which had evidently gone out. There was no sign of Heather. The night was perfectly quiet except for the sound of our breathing. And the crickets.

That's how I knew Heather was really gone. The crickets had started up again.

"Jesus," Sleepy said again, still panting pretty heavily, "are you sure you're all right, Suze?"

I turned to look at him. All he had on was a pair of jeans and an Army jacket, thrown hastily over a bare chest. Sleepy, I noticed, had almost as defined a six-pack as Jesse.

How is it that I'd nearly been smothered to death, and yet I could sit there and notice things like my stepbrother's abdominal muscles a few minutes later?

"Yeah," I said, pushing some hair out of my eyes. "I'm fine. A little banged up, maybe. But nothing broken."

"She should probably go to the hospital and get checked out." David's voice was still pretty wobbly. "Don't you think she should go to the hospital and get checked out, Jake?"

"No," I said. "No hospitals."

"You could have a concussion," David said. "Or a fractured skull. You might slip into a coma in your sleep and never wake up. You should at least get an X ray. Or an MRI, maybe. A CAT scan wouldn't hurt, either—"

"No." I brushed my hands off on my leggings and stood up. My body felt pretty creaky, but whole. "Come on. Let's get out of here before somebody comes. They were bound to have heard all that." I nodded toward the part of the building where the priests and nuns lived. Lights had come on in some of the windows. "I don't want to get you guys in trouble."

"Yeah," Sleepy said, getting up. "Well, you might have thought of that before you snuck out, huh?"

We left the way we'd come in. Like me, David had wriggled in beneath the front gate, then unlocked it from the inside and let Sleepy in. We slipped out as quietly as we could, and hurried to the Rambler, which Sleepy had parked in some shadows, out of sight of the police car. The black-and-white was still sitting there, its occupant perfectly oblivious to what had gone on just a few dozen yards away. Still, I didn't want to risk anything by trying to sneak past him, and retrieve my bike. We just left it there, and hoped no one would notice it.

The whole way home, my new big brother Jake lectured me. Apparently, he thought I'd been at the school in the middle of the night as part of some sort of gang initiation. I kid you not. He was really very indignant about the whole thing. He wanted to know what kind of friends I thought these people were, leaving me to die under a pile of roofing tiles. He suggested that if I were bored or in need of a thrill, I should take up surfing because, and I quote, "If you're gonna have your head split open, it might as well be while you're riding a wave, dude."

I took his lecture as gracefully as I could. After all, I couldn't very well tell him the real reason I'd been down at the school after hours. I only interrupted Jake once during his little antigang speech, and that was to ask him just how he and David had known to come after me.

"I don't know," Jake said, as we pulled up the driveway. "All I know is, I was catching some pretty heavy-duty Z's, when all of a sudden Dave is all over me, telling me we have to go down to the school and find you. How'd you know she was down there, anyway, Dave?"

David's face was unnaturally white even in the moonlight. "I don't know," he said quietly. "I just had a feeling."

I turned to look at him, hard. But he wouldn't meet my eye.

*That kid*, I thought. *That kid knows.*

But I was too tired to talk about it just then. We snuck into the house, relieved that the only occupant who woke upon our entrance was Max, who wagged his tail and tried to lick us as we made our way to our rooms. Before I slipped into mine, I looked over at David just once, to see if he wanted—or needed—to say anything to me. But he didn't. He just went into his room and shut his door, a scared little boy. My heart swelled for him.

But only for a second. I was too tired to think of anything much but bed—not even Jesse. *In the morning,* I told myself, as I peeled off my dusty clothes. *I'll talk to him in the morning.*

I didn't, though. When I woke up, the light outside my windows looked funny. When I lifted my head and saw the clock, I realized why. It was two o'clock in the afternoon. All the morning fog had burned away, and the sun was beating down as hard as if it were July and not January.

"Well, hey there, sleepyhead."

I squinted in the direction of my bedroom door. Andy stood there, leaning against the doorframe with his arms folded across his chest. He was grinning, which meant I probably wasn't in trouble. What was I doing in bed at two o'clock in the afternoon on a school day, then?

"Feeling better?" Andy wanted to know.

I pushed the bedcovers down a little. Was I supposed to be sick? Well, that wouldn't be hard to fake. I felt as if someone had dropped a ton of bricks on my head.

Which, in a way, I suppose they had.

"Uh," I said. "Not really."

"I'll get you some aspirin. I guess it all caught up with you, huh? The jet lag, I mean. When we couldn't wake you up this morning, we decided just to let you sleep. Your mom said to tell you she's sorry, but she had to go to work. She put me in charge. Hope you don't mind."

I tried to sit up. It was really hard. Every muscle in my body felt as if it had been pounded on. I pushed some hair out of my eyes and blinked at him. "You didn't have to," I said. "Stay home on my account, I mean."

Andy shrugged. "It's no big deal. I've barely had a chance to talk to you since you got here, so I thought we could catch up. You want some lunch?"

The minute he said it, my stomach growled. I was starving.

He heard it and grinned. "No problem. Get dressed and come on downstairs. We'll have lunch on the deck. It's really beautiful out today."

I dragged myself out of bed with an effort. I had my pj's on. I didn't feel very much like getting dressed. So I just pulled on some socks and a bathrobe, brushed my teeth, and stood for a minute by the bay windows, looking out as I tried to work the snarls out of my hair. The red dome of the Mission church glowed in the sunlight. I could see the ocean winking behind it. You couldn't tell from up here that it had been the scene last night of so much destruction.

It wasn't long before an extremely appetizing aroma rose up from the kitchen and lured me down the stairs. Andy was making Reuben sandwiches. He waved me out of the kitchen, though, toward the huge deck he'd built onto the back of the house. The sun was pouring down there, and I stretched out on one of the padded chaise longues, and pretended like I was a movie star for a while. Then Andy came out with the sandwiches and a pitcher of lemonade, and I moved to the table with the big green umbrella over it, and dug in. For a non–New Yorker, Andy grilled a mean Reuben.

And that wasn't all he grilled. He spent a half hour grilling me pretty thoroughly . . . but not about what had happened the night before. To my astonishment, Sleepy and Doc had kept their mouths shut. Andy was perfectly in the dark about what had happened. All he wanted to know was whether I liked my new school, if I was happy, blah, blah, blah . . . .

Except for one thing. He did say to me, as he was asking me how I liked California, and was it really so very different from New York—uh, duh—"So, I guess you slept straight through your first earthquake."

I nearly choked on a chip. "What?"

"Your first quake. There was one last night, around two in the morning. Not a big one, really—round about a four pointer—but it woke *me* up. No damage, except down at the Mission, evidently. Breezeway collapsed. But then, that should come as no surprise to them. I've been warning them for years about that timber. It's nearly as old as the Mission itself. Can't be expected to last forever."

I chewed more carefully. Wow. Heather's goodbye bang must have really packed a wallop if people all over the Valley, and even up in the hills, had felt it.

But that still didn't explain how David had known to look for me down at the school.

I'd moved upstairs and was sitting on the window seat in my room flipping through a mindless fashion magazine, wondering where Jesse had gone off to, and how long I was going to have to wait before he showed up to give me another one of his lectures, and if there was any chance he might call me *querida* again, when the boys got home from school. Dopey stomped right past my room—he still blamed me for getting him grounded—but Sleepy poked his head in, looked at me, saw that I was all right, then went away, shaking his head. Only David knocked, and when I called for him to come in, did so, shyly.

"Um," he said. "I brought you your homework. Mr. Walden gave it to me to give to you. He said he hoped you were feeling better."

"Oh," I said. "Thanks, David. Just put it down there on the bed."

David did so, but he didn't go. He just stood there staring at the bedpost. I figured he needed to talk, so I decided to let him by not saying anything myself.

"CeeCee says hi," he said. "And that other kid. Adam McTavish."

"That's nice of them," I said.

I waited. David did not disappoint.

"Everybody's talking about it, you know," he said.

"Talking about what?"

"You know. The quake. That the Mission must be over some fault no one ever knew about before, since the epicenter seemed to be . . . seemed to be right next to Mr. Walden's classroom."

I said, "Huh," and turned the page of my magazine.

"So," David said. "You're never going to tell me, are you?"

I didn't look at him. "Tell you what?"

"What's going on. Why you were down at the school in the middle of the night. How that breezeway came down. Any of it."

"It's better that you don't know," I said, flipping the page. "Trust me."

"But it doesn't have to do with . . . with what Jake said. With a gang. Does it?"

"No," I said.

I looked at him then. The sun, pouring through my windows, brought out the pink highlights in his skin. This boy—this redheaded boy with the sticky-outy ears—had saved my life. I owed him an explanation, at the very least.

"I saw it, you know," David said.

"Saw what?"

"It. The ghost."

He was staring at me, white-faced and intent. He looked way too serious for a twelve-year-old.

"What ghost?" I asked.

"The one who lives here. In this room." He glanced around, as if expecting to see Jesse looming in one of the corners of my bright, sunny room. "It came to me, last night," he said. "I swear it. It woke me up. It told me about you.

That's how I knew. That's how I knew you were in trouble."

I stared at him with my mouth hanging open. *Jesse? Jesse* had told him? *Jesse* had woken him up?

"It wouldn't let me alone," David said, his voice trembling. "It kept on . . . touching me. My shoulder. It was cold and it glowed. It was just a cold, glowing thing, and inside my head there was this voice telling me I had to get down to the school and help you. I'm not lying, Suze. I swear it really happened."

"I know it did, David," I said, closing the magazine. "I believe you."

He'd opened his mouth to swear it was true some more, but when I told him I believed him, his jaw clicked shut. He only opened it again to say wonderingly, "You *do*?"

"I do," I said. "I didn't get a chance last night to say it, so I'll say it now. Thank you, David. You and Jake saved my life."

He was shaking. He had to sit down on my bed, or he probably would have fallen down.

"So . . ." he said. "So it's true. It really was . . . the ghost?"

"It really was."

He digested that. "And why were you down at the school?"

"It's a long story," I said. "But I promise you, it doesn't have anything to do with gangs."

He blinked at me. "Does it have to do with . . . the ghost?"

"Not the one who visited you. But yes, it had to do with a ghost."

David's lips moved, but I don't think he was really aware he was speaking. What came out of his mouth was an astonished, "There's more than one?"

"Oh, there's *way* more than one," I said.

He stared at me some more. "And you . . . you can see them?"

"David," I said. "This isn't really something I'm all that comfortable discussing—"

"Have you seen the one from last night? The one who woke me up?"

"Yes, David. I've seen him."

"Do you know who he is? How he died, I mean?"

I shook my head. "No. Remember? You were going to look it up for me."

David brightened. "Oh, yeah! I forgot. I checked some books out yesterday—stay here a minute. Don't go anywhere."

He ran from the room, all of his recent shock forgotten. I stayed where I was, exactly as he'd told me to. I wondered if Jesse was somewhere nearby, listening. I figured it would serve him right if he were.

David was back in a flash, bringing with him a large pile of dusty, oversize books. They looked really ancient, and when he sat down beside me and eagerly began leafing through them, I saw that they were every bit as old as they looked. None of them had been published after 1910. The oldest had been published in 1849.

"Look," David said, flipping through a large, leather-bound volume entitled *My Monterey. My Monterey* had been written by one Colonel Harold Clemmings. The colonel had a rather dry narrative style, but there were pictures to look at, which helped, even if they were in black and white.

"Look," David said again, turning to a reproduction of a photograph of the house we were sitting in. Only the house looked a good deal different, having no porch and no carport. Also, the trees around it were much smaller. "Look, see, here's the house when it was a hotel. Or a boardinghouse, as they called it back then. It says here the house had a pretty bad reputation. A lot of people were murdered here. Colonel Clemmings goes into detail about all of them. Do you suppose the ghost who came to me last night is one of them? One of the people who died here, I mean?"

"Well," I said. "Most likely."

David began reading out loud—quickly and intelligently, and without stumbling over the big, old-fashioned words—the different stories of people who had died in what Colonel Clemmings referred to as the House in the Hills.

None of those people, however, was named Jesse. None of them sounded even remotely like him. When David was through, he looked up at me hopefully.

"Maybe the ghost belongs to that Chinese launderer," he said. "The one who was shot because he didn't wash that dandy's shirts fine enough."

I shook my head. "No. Our ghost isn't Chinese."

"Oh." David consulted the book again. "How about this guy? The guy who was killed by his slaves?"

"I don't think so," I said. "He was only five feet tall."

"Well, what about this guy? This Dane who they caught cheating at cards, and blew away?"

"He's not Danish," I said with a sigh.

David pursed his lips. "Well, what was he, then? This ghost?'

I shook my head. "I don't know. At least part

Spanish. And . . ." I didn't want to go into it right there in my room, where Jesse might overhear. You know, about his liquid eyes and long brown fingers and all that.

I mean, I didn't want him to think that I *liked* him or anything.

Then I remembered the handkerchief. It had been gone when I'd woken up the next morning, after I'd washed my blood out of it, but I still remembered the initials. MDS. I told them to David. "Do those letters mean anything to you?"

He looked thoughtful for a minute. Then he closed Colonel Clemmings's book and picked up another one. This one was even older and dustier. It was so old, the title had rubbed off the spine. But when David opened it, I saw by the title page that it was called *Life in Northern California, 1800–1850.*

David scanned the index in the back, and then went, "Aha."

"Aha what?" I asked.

"Aha, I thought so," David said. He flipped to a page toward the end. "Here," he said. "I knew it. There's a picture of her." He handed me the book, and I saw a page with a layer of tissue over it.

"What's this?" I said. "There's Kleenex in this book."

"It isn't Kleenex. It's tissue. They used to put that over pictures in books to protect them. Lift it up."

I lifted up the tissue. Underneath it was a black-and-white copy on glossy paper of a painting. The painting was a portrait of a woman. Underneath the woman's portrait were the words MARIA DE SILVA DIEGO, 1830–1916.

My jaw dropped. *MDS!* Maria de Silva!

She looked like the type that would have a handkerchief like that tucked up her sleeve. She was dressed in a frilly white thing—at least, it looked white in the black-and-white picture—with her shiny black hair all ringleted on either side of her head, and a big old expensive-looking jewel hanging from a gold chain around her long neck. A beautiful, proud-looking woman, she stared out of the frame of the portrait with an expression you just had to call . . . well, contemptuous.

I looked at David. "Who was she?" I asked.

"Oh, just the most popular girl in California at around the time this house was built." David took the book away from me, and flipped through it. "Her father, Ricardo de Silva, owned most of Salinas back then. She was his only daughter, and he settled a pretty hefty dowry on her. That's not why people wanted to marry her, though. Well, not the only reason. Back then, people actually considered girls who looked like that beautiful."

I said, "She's *very* beautiful."

David glanced at me with a funny little smile. "Yeah," he said. "Right."

"No. She really is."

David saw I was serious, and shrugged. "Well, whatever. Her dad wanted her to marry this rich rancher—some cousin of hers who was madly in love with her—but she was all into this other guy, this guy named Diego." He consulted the book. "Felix Diego. This guy was bad news. He was a slave runner. At least, that's what he'd done for a living before he came out to California to strike it rich in the gold mines. And Maria's dad, he didn't approve of slavery, any more than he approved of gold diggers. So Maria and her dad, they had this big fight about it—who she was going to marry, I mean, the cousin or the slave runner—until finally, her dad said he was going to cut her off if she didn't marry the cousin. That shut Maria up pretty quick because she was a girl who liked money a lot. She had something like sixty dresses back when most women had two, one for work and one for church—"

"So what happened?" I interrupted. I didn't

care how many dresses the woman owned. I wanted to know where Jesse came in.

"Oh." David consulted the book. "Well, the funny thing is, after all that, Maria won out in the end."

"How?"

"The cousin never showed up for the wedding."

I blinked at him. "Never showed up? What do you mean, he never showed up?"

"That's just it. He never showed up. Nobody knows what happened to him. He left his ranch a few days before the wedding, you know, so he'd get there on time or whatever, but then nobody heard from him again. Ever. The end."

"And . . ." I knew the answer, but I had to ask, anyway. "And what happened to Maria?"

"Oh, she married the gold-digging slave runner. I mean, after they'd waited a decent interval and all. There were all these rules back then about that kind of thing. Her dad was so disappointed, you know, that the cousin had turned out to be so unreliable, that he finally just told Maria she could do whatever she wanted, and be damned. So she did. But she wasn't damned. She and the slave runner had eleven kids and took over her father's properties after he died and did a pretty good job running them—"

I held up my hand. "Wait. What was the cousin's name?"

David consulted the book. "Hector."

*"Hector?"*

"Yes." David looked back down at the book. "Hector de Silva. His mom called him Jesse, though."

When he looked back up, he must have seen something in my face since he went, in a small voice, "Is that our ghost?"

"That," I said softly, "is our ghost."

# chapter *nineteen*

The phone rang a little while later. Dopey yelled down the hall that it was for me. I picked up, and heard CeeCee squealing on the other end of the line.

"Ms. Vice President," she said. "Ms. Vice President, do you have any comment?"

I said, "No, and why are you calling me Ms. Vice President?"

"Because you won the election." In the background, I heard Adam shout, "Congratulations!"

"What election?" I asked, baffled.

"For vice president!" CeeCee sounded annoyed. "Duh!"

"How could I have won it?" I said. "I wasn't even there."

"That's okay. You still won two-thirds of the sophomore class's vote."

*"Two-thirds?"* I'll admit it. That shocked me. "But, CeeCee—I mean, why did people vote for *me?* They don't even *know* me. I'm the new kid."

CeeCee said, "What can I say? You exude the confidence of a born leader."

"But—"

"And it probably doesn't hurt that you're from New York, and around here, people are fascinated by anything to do with New York."

"But—"

"And, of course, you talk really fast."

"I do?"

"Sure you do. And that makes you seem smart. I mean, *I* think you *are* smart, but you also *seem* smart because you talk really fast. And you wear a lot of black, and black is, you know, cool."

"But—"

"Oh, and the fact that you saved Bryce from that falling chunk of wood. People like that kind of thing."

Two-thirds of the sophomore class at Mission High School, I thought, would probably have voted for the Easter Bunny if someone could have gotten him to run for office. But I didn't say so. Instead, I said, "Well. Neat. I guess."

"Neat?" CeeCee sounded stunned. "*Neat?* That's all you have to say, *neat*? Do you have any idea how much fun we're going to have now that we've managed to get our hands on all that money? The cool things we'll be able to do?"

I said, "I guess that's really . . . great."

"Great? Suze, it's *awesome*! We are going to have an awesome, awesome semester! I'm so proud of you! And to think, I knew you when!"

I hung up the phone feeling a little overwhelmed. It isn't every day a girl gets elected vice president of a class she's been in for less than a week.

I hadn't even put the phone back into its cradle before it rang again. This time it was a girl's voice I didn't recognize, asking to speak to Suze Simon.

"This is she," I said, and Kelly Prescott shrieked in my ear.

"Omigod!" she cried. "Have you heard? Aren't you psyched? We are going to have a *bitching* year."

Bitching. All right. I said calmly, "I look forward to working with you."

"Look," Kelly said, suddenly all business. "We have to get together soon and choose the music."

"The music for what?"

"For the dance, of course." I could hear her flipping through an organizer. "I've got a DJ all lined up. He sent me a playlist, and we have to choose what songs for him to play. How's tomorrow night? What's wrong with you, anyway? You weren't in school today. You're not contagious, are you?"

I said, "Um, no. Listen, Kelly, about this dance. I don't know about it. I was thinking it might be more fun to spend the money on . . . well, something like a beach cookout."

She said in a perfectly flat tone of voice, "A beach cookout."

"Yeah. With volleyball and a bonfire and stuff." I twisted the phone cord around my finger. "After we have Heather's memorial, of course."

"Heather's what?"

"Her memorial service. See, I figure you already booked the room at the Carmel Inn, right, for the dance? But instead of having a dance there, I think we should have a memorial service for Heather. I really think, you know, she'd have wanted it that way."

Kelly's tone was flat. "You never even met Heather."

"Well," I said. "That may be. But I have a pretty

good feeling I know what type of girl she was. And I think a memorial service at the Carmel Inn would be exactly what she'd want."

Kelly didn't say anything for a minute. Well, it had occurred to me she might not like my suggestions, but she couldn't really do anything about it now, could she? After all, I was the vice president. And I don't think, short of expulsion from the Mission Academy, I could be impeached.

"Kelly?" When she didn't answer, I said, "Well, look, Kell, don't worry about it now. We'll talk. Oh, and about your pool party on Saturday. I hope you don't mind, but I asked CeeCee and Adam to come. You know, it's funny, but they say they didn't get invited. But in a class as small as ours, it really isn't fair not to invite everybody, you know what I mean? Otherwise, the people who didn't get invited might think you don't like them. But I'm sure in CeeCee's and Adam's cases, you just forgot, right?"

Kelly went, "Are you mental?"

I chose not to dignify that with a response. "See you tomorrow, Kell," was all I said.

A few minutes later, the phone rang again. I picked up, since it appeared I was on a winning streak. And I wasn't wrong. It was Father Dominic.

"Susannah," he said in his pleasantly deep voice. "I do hope you don't mind my bothering you at home. But I just called to congratulate you on winning the sophomore class—"

"Don't worry, Father Dom," I said. "No one's on the other extension. It's only me."

"What," he said, in a completely different tone of voice, "could you have been thinking? You promised me! You promised me you wouldn't go back to the school grounds alone!"

"I'm sorry," I said. "But she was threatening to hurt David, and I—"

"I don't care if she was threatening your mother, young lady. Next time, you are to wait for me. Do you understand? Never again are you to attempt something so foolhardy and dangerous as an exorcism without a soul to help you!"

I said, "Well, okay. But I was kind of hoping there wasn't going to be a next time."

"Not be a next time? Are you daft? We're mediators, remember. So long as there are spirits, there will be a next time for us, young lady, and don't you forget it."

As if I could. All I had to do was look around my bedroom just about any time of day, and there was my very own reminder, in the form of a murdered cowboy.

But I didn't see any point in telling Father Dominic this. Instead, I said, "Sorry about your breezeway, Father Dominic. Your poor birds."

"Never mind my birds. You're all right, and that's all that matters. When I get out of this hospital, you and I are going to sit down and have a very long chat, Susannah, about proper mediation techniques. I don't know about this habit of yours of just walking up and punching the poor souls in the face."

I said, laughing, "Okay. I guess your ribs must be hurting you, huh?"

He said in a gentler tone, "They are, some. How did you know?"

"Because you're so pleasant."

"I'm sorry." Father Dominic actually sounded it, too. "I—yes, my ribs *are* hurting me. Oh, Susannah. Did you hear the news?"

"Which? That I was voted sophomore class vice president, or that I wrecked the school last night?"

"Neither. A space has been found at Robert Louis Stevenson High School for Bryce. He'll be transferring there just as soon as he can walk again."

"But—" It was ridiculous, I know, but I actually felt dismayed. "But Heather's gone now. He doesn't have to transfer."

"Heather may be gone," Father Dominic said gently, "but her memory still exists very much in the minds of those who were . . . affected by her death. Surely you can't blame the boy for wanting a chance to start over at a new school where people won't be whispering about him?"

I said, not very graciously, thinking of Bryce's soft blond hair, "I guess."

"They say I should be well enough to return to work Monday. Shall I see you in my office then?"

"I guess," I said, just as enthusiastically as before. Father Dominic didn't appear to notice. He said, "I shall see you then." Right before I hung up, I heard him say, "Oh, and Susannah. Do try, in the interim, not to destroy what's left of the school."

"Ha-ha," I said, and hung up.

Sitting on the window seat, I rested my chin on my knees and gazed down across the valley toward the curve of the bay. The sun was starting to sink low in the west. It hadn't hit the water yet, but it would in a few minutes. My room was ablaze with reds and golds, and the sky around the sun looked as if it were striped. The clouds were so many different colors—blue and purple and red and orange—like the ribbons I once saw waving from the top of a maypole at a Renaissance fair. I could smell the sea, too, through my open window. The breeze carried the briny scent toward me, even as high up in the hills as I was.

Had Jesse, I wondered, sat in this window and smelled the ocean like I was doing, before he died? Before—as I was sure had happened—Maria de Silva's lover, Felix Diego, slipped into the room and killed him?

As if he'd read my thoughts, Jesse suddenly materialized a few feet away from me.

"Jeez!" I said, pressing a hand over my heart, which was beating so hard I thought it might explode. "Do you have to keep on *doing* that?"

He was leaning, sort of nonchalantly, against one of my bedposts, his arms folded across his chest. "I'm sorry," he said. But he didn't look it.

"Look," I said. "If you and I are going to be living together—so to speak—we need to come up with some rules. And rule number one is that you have got to stop sneaking up on me like that."

"And how do you suggest I make my presence known?" Jesse asked, his eyes pretty bright for a ghost.

"I don't know," I said. "Can't you rattle some chains or something?"

He shook his head. "I don't think so. What would rule number two be?"

"Rule number two . . ." My voice trailed off as I stared at him. It wasn't fair. It really wasn't. Dead guys should not look anywhere near as good as Jesse looked, leaning there against my bedpost with the sun slanting in and catching the perfectly sculpted planes of his face. . . .

He lifted that eyebrow, the one with the scar in it. "Something wrong, *querida*?" he asked.

I stared at him. It was clear he didn't know that I knew. About MDS, I mean. I wanted to ask him about it, but in another way, I sort of didn't want to know. Something was keeping Jesse in this world and out of the one he belonged to, and I had a feeling that something was directly related to the manner in which he'd lost his life. But since he didn't seem all that anxious to talk about it, I figured it was none of my business.

This was a first. Most times, ghosts were all over me to help them. But not Jesse.

At least, not for now.

"Let me ask you something," Jesse said so suddenly that I thought, for a minute, maybe he'd read my mind.

"What?" I asked cautiously, throwing down my magazine and standing up.

"Last night, when you warned me not to go near the school because you were doing an exorcism . . ."

I eyed him. "Yes?"

"Why did you warn me?"

I laughed with relief. Was that all? "I warned you because if you'd gone down there you would have been sucked away just like Heather."

"But wouldn't that have been a perfect way to get rid of me? You'd have this room to yourself, just the way you want it."

I stared at him in horror. "But that—that would have been completely unfair!"

He was smiling now. "I see. Against the rules?"

"Yeah," I said. "Big time."

"Then you didn't warn me"—he took a step toward me—"because you're starting to like me or anything like that?"

Much to my dismay, I felt my face start to heat up. "No," I said stubbornly. "Nothing like that. I'm just trying to play by the rules. Which you violated, by the way, when you woke up David."

Jesse took another step toward me. "I had to. You'd warned me not to go down to the school myself. What choice did I have? If I hadn't sent your brother in my place to help you," he pointed out, "you'd be a bit dead now."

I was uncomfortably aware that this was true. However, I wasn't about to let on that I agreed with him. "No way," I said. "I had things perfectly under control. I—"

"You had nothing under control." Jesse laughed. "You went barreling in there without any sort of plan, without any sort of—"

"I had a plan." I took a single furious step toward him, and suddenly we were standing practically nose to nose. "Who do you think you are, telling me I had no plan? I've been doing this for years, get it? Years. And I never needed help, not from anyone. And certainly not from someone like *you*."

He stopped laughing suddenly. Now he looked mad. "Someone like me? You mean—what was it you called me? A cowboy?"

"No," I said. "I mean from somebody who's *dead*."

Jesse flinched, almost as violently as if I'd hit him.

"Let's make rule number two be that from now on, you stay out of my business, and I'll stay out of yours," I said.

"Fine," Jesse said shortly.

"Fine," I said. "And thank you."

He was still mad. He asked sullenly, "For what?"

"For saving my life."

He stopped looking mad all of a sudden. His eyebrows, which had been all knit together, relaxed.

Next thing I knew, he'd reached out, and laid his hands on my shoulders.

If he'd stuck a fork in me, I don't think I'd have been so surprised. I mean, I'm used to punching ghosts in the face. I am not used to them looking down at me as if . . . as if . . .

Well, as if they were about to kiss me.

But before I had time to figure out what I was going to do—close my eyes and let him do it, or invoke rule number three: absolutely no touching—my mother's voice drifted up from downstairs. "Susannah?" she called. "Susie, it's Mom. I'm home."

I looked at Jesse. He jerked his hands away from me. A second later, my mom opened my bedroom door, and Jesse disappeared.

"Susie," she said. She walked over and put her arms around me. "How are you? I hope you're not upset that we let you sleep in. You just seemed so tired."

"No," I said. I was still sort of dazed by what had happened with Jesse. "I don't mind."

"I guess it all finally caught up with you. I

thought it might. Were you all right here with Andy? He said he made you lunch."

"He made me a fine lunch," I said automatically.

"And David brought you your homework, I hear." She let go of me and walked toward the window seat. "We were thinking about spaghetti for dinner. What do you think?"

"Sounds good." I came around long enough to notice that she was staring out of the windows. Then I noticed that I couldn't remember my mother ever looking so . . . well, serene.

Maybe it was the fact that since we'd moved out west, she'd given up coffee.

More likely, though, it was love.

"What are you looking at, Mom?" I asked her.

"Oh, nothing, honey," she said with a little smile. "Just the sunset. It's so beautiful." She turned to put her arm around me, and together we stood there and watched the sun sinking into the Pacific in a blaze of violent reds and purples and golds. "You sure wouldn't see a sunset like that back in New York," my mother said. "Now would you?"

"No," I said. "You wouldn't."

"So," she said, giving me a squeeze. "What do you think? You think we should stick around here awhile?"

She was joking, of course. But in a way, she wasn't.

"Sure," I said. "We should stick around."

She smiled at me, then turned back toward the sunset. The last of the bright orange ball was disappearing beneath the horizon. "There goes the sun," she said.

"And," I said, "it's all right."

Suze's supernatural misadventures
continue in the second Mediator book,

# Ninth Key

The following is an excerpt:

The first time she showed up, it was about an hour after I'd come home from the pool party. Around three in the morning, I guess. And what she did was, she stood by my bed and started screaming.

*Really* screaming. *Really* loud. She woke me out of a dead sleep. I'd been lying there dreaming about Bryce Martinson. In my dream, he and I were cruising along Seventeen Mile Drive in this red convertible. I don't know whose convertible it was. His, I guess, since I don't even have my driver's license yet. Bryce's soft sandy-blond hair was blowing in the wind, and the sun was sinking into the sea, making the sky all red and orange and purple. We were going around these curves, you know, on the cliffs above the Pacific, and I wasn't even carsick or anything. It was one really terrific dream.

And then this woman starts wailing, practically in my ear.

I ask you: Who needs that?

Of course I sat up right away, completely wide awake. Having a walking dead woman show up in your bedroom screaming her head off can do that to you. Wake you up right away, I mean.

I sat there blinking because my room was really dark—well, it was nighttime. You know, nighttime, when normal people are asleep.

But not us mediators. Oh, no.

She was standing in this skinny patch of moonlight coming in from the bay windows on the far side of my room. She had on a gray hooded sweatshirt, hood down, a T-shirt, capri pants, and Keds. Her hair was short, sort of mousy brown. It was hard to tell if she was young or old, what with all the screaming and everything, but I kind of figured her for my mom's age.

Which was why I didn't get out of bed and punch her right then and there.

I probably should have. I mean, it wasn't like I could exactly yell back at her, not without waking the whole house. I was the only one in the house who could hear her.

Well, the only one who was alive, anyway.

After a while, I guess she noticed I was awake

because she stopped screaming and reached up to wipe her eyes. She was crying pretty hard.

"I'm sorry," she said.

I said, "Yeah, well, you got my attention. Now what do you want?"

"I need you," she said. She was sniffling. "I need you to tell someone something."

I said, "Okay. What?"

"Tell him . . ." She wiped her face with her hands. "Tell him it wasn't his fault. He didn't kill me."

This was sort of a new one. I raised my eyebrows. "Tell him he *didn't* kill you?" I asked, just to be sure I'd heard her right.

She nodded. She was kind of pretty, I guess, in a waifish sort of way. Although it probably wouldn't have hurt if she'd eaten a muffin or two back when she'd been alive.

"You'll tell him?" she asked me, eagerly. "Promise?"

"Sure," I said. "I'll tell him. Only who am I telling?"

She looked at me funny. "Red, of course."

*Red?* Was she *kidding*?

But it was too late. She was gone.

Just like that.

Red. I turned around and beat on my pillow to

get it fluffy again. Red.

Why me? I mean, really. To be interrupted while having a dream about Bryce Martinson just because some woman wants a guy named *Red* to know he *didn't* kill her. . . . I swear, sometimes I am convinced my life is just a series of sketches for *America's Funniest Home Videos,* minus all that pants-dropping business.

Except my life really isn't all that funny if you think about it.

I especially wasn't laughing when, the minute I finally found a comfy spot on my pillow and was just about to close my eyes and go back to sleep, somebody else showed up in the sliver of moonlight in the middle of my room.

This time there wasn't any screaming. That was about the only thing I had to be grateful for.

*"What?"* I asked in a pretty rude voice.

He said, shaking his head, "You didn't even ask her name."

I leaned up on both elbows. It was because of this guy that I'd taken to wearing a T-shirt and boxer shorts to bed. Not that I had been going around in floaty negligees before he'd come along, but I sure wasn't going to take them up now that I had a male roommate.

Yeah, you read that right.

"Like she gave me the chance," I said.

"You could have asked." Jesse folded his arms across his chest. "But you didn't bother."

"Excuse me," I said, sitting up. "This is *my* bedroom. I will treat spectral visitors to it any way I want to, thank you."

He said, "Susannah."

He had the softest voice imaginable. Softer, even, than that guy Tad's. It was like silk or something, his voice. It was really hard to be mean to a guy with a voice like that.

But the thing was, I *had* to be mean. Because even in the moonlight, I could make out the breadth of his strong shoulders, the vee where his old-fashioned white shirt fell open, revealing dark, olive-complected skin, some chest hair, and just about the best-defined abs you've ever seen. I could also see the strong planes of his face, the tiny scar in one of his ink-black eyebrows, where something—or someone—had cut him once.

Kelly Prescott was wrong. Bryce Martinson was not the cutest guy in Carmel.

Jesse was.

*Read all the Mediator books:*

THE MEDIATOR 1:
*Shadowland*

THE MEDIATOR 2:

*Ninth Key*

THE MEDIATOR 3:
*Reunion*

THE MEDIATOR 4:
*Darkest Hour*

THE MEDIATOR 5:
*Haunted*

THE MEDIATOR 6:
*Twilight*

*Meg Cabot* is also the author of the Princess Diaries series, upon which the Disney movies are based. In the books, though, Princess Mia has yield-sign-shaped hair, lives in New York, and Fat Louie is orange. And those are the least of the differences. The following is a complete list of the Princess Diaries books:

THE PRINCESS DIARIES

THE PRINCESS DIARIES, VOLUME II:
PRINCESS IN THE SPOTLIGHT

THE PRINCESS DIARIES, VOLUME III:
PRINCESS IN LOVE

THE PRINCESS DIARIES, VOLUME IV:
PRINCESS IN WAITING

THE PRINCESS DIARIES, VOLUME IV AND A HALF:
PROJECT PRINCESS

THE PRINCESS DIARIES, VOLUME V:
PRINCESS IN PINK

THE PRINCESS DIARIES, VOLUME VI:
PRINCESS IN TRAINING

THE PRINCESS PRESENT:
A PRINCESS DIARIES BOOK

PRINCESS LESSONS:
A PRINCESS DIARIES BOOK

PERFECT PRINCESS:
A PRINCESS DIARIES BOOK

Aside from the Mediator books
and the Princess Diaries books, Meg
has written several more books:

## ALL-AMERICAN GIRL

Samantha Madison saves the president's life . . . only to have his son fall in love with her. Which would be fine, except for all the Secret Service agents following them around.

## teen IDOL

Jenny Greenley gives everyone advice, so why can't she follow her own and find love? Further complicating matters is the presence of hot Hollywood star Luke Striker in Jenny's homeroom, of all places.

## Nicola and the Viscount

It's 1810, and Nicola Sparks is ready to dive headlong into her first London Season. Good thing there's a handsome viscount there to catch her!

## Victoria and the Rogue

Lady Victoria Arbuthnot is accustomed to being right. She isn't always, though, especially when her own heart is concerned.

*But wait!*
*There's more by Meg:*

THE BOY NEXT DOOR

BOY MEETS GIRL

EVERY BOY'S GOT ONE

THE 1-800-WHERE-R-YOU BOOKS:

WHEN LIGHTNING STRIKES

CODE NAME CASSANDRA

SAFE HOUSE

SANCTUARY

*For more about Meg and to read her diary, visit:*

**www.megcabot.com**

*Join her online book club at:*

**www.megcabotbookclub.com**